THE TAYLORS

JEN CALONITA

SCHOLASTIC

Published in the UK by Scholastic, 2025
Scholastic, Bosworth Avenue, Warwick, CV34 6UQ
Scholastic Ireland, 89E Lagan Road, Dublin Industrial Estate, Glasnevin, Dublin, D11 HP5F

SCHOLASTIC and associated logos are trademarks and/or
registered trademarks of Scholastic Inc.

First published in the US by Scholastic Inc., 2025

Text © Jen Calonita, 2025
Interior art by Liz Parkes © Scholastic Inc., 2025

Book design by Stephanie Yang

The moral rights of the author have been asserted by them.

ISBN 978 0702 34338 4

A CIP catalogue record for this book is available from the British Library.

Printed in the UK
Paper made from wood grown in sustainable forests and other controlled sources.

MIX
Paper | Supporting
responsible forestry
FSC® C018072

10 9 8 7 6 5 4 3 2 1

FOR ELPIDA ARGENZIANO. THANK YOU FOR BEING THE WORLD'S BEST FRIEND, AND FOR MAKING ME YOUR PLUS-ONE FOR THE ERAS TOUR.

THE TAYLORS

Teffy

Taylor

Tay Tay

TS

ONE

Would've, Could've, Should've

Taylor Bennett was pretty sure today was going to be the worst day of her life.

How could it not be?

It was her first day at Harrison Middle School and she didn't know a single person in her homeroom class.

Not one.

"I can do this, right?" she asked the woman in the picture taped to her bedroom mirror. "Go to middle school and sit in class with kids I don't know and make friends? What's so hard about that?"

She paused for a moment, letting that thought sink in as she slipped several colorful friendship bracelets onto her right wrist. Then she thought about how hard it was to make friends in her class last year and her heart started to beat like a drum. "Nope. I can't do this. I lied. I want to be homeschooled."

"Teffy! You're going to be late! Let's go!" her mom yelled up the stairs.

(Her mom had good lungs. Teffy could hear her from anywhere in the house, even when she was wearing earbuds.)

"Coming!" Teffy yelled back.

Teffy was Taylor's nickname. Everyone in her family had been calling her Teffy since her brother, Charlie, learned that was what Taylor Swift's brother, Austin, called his sister. Teffy came from a family of Swifties. Her parents had named her Taylor after the singer and her dad had picked her middle name, Elizabeth, for Elizabeth Bennet, a character from *Pride and Prejudice*, one of her dad's favorite books. Was it her genes coupled with her namesakes that had led Teffy to being both a Swiftie and an avid reader? Maybe. Teffy liked to think that, like her parents, she had good taste.

She was also secretly hopeful some of Taylor's confidence would eventually rub off on her. Teffy hated how shy she was, but she couldn't help it. Her worst fear was small talk, so making friends had always been difficult. And from the way Charlie explained it, middle school was going to mean everything got a whole lot harder.

"Guess asking Mom if I can be homeschooled is out since the first day of school starts in an hour." Teffy put down her glitter hairbrush that sometimes doubled as a microphone. "I wish I wasn't so nervous."

You're not *on your own, kid. You can face this*, the picture seemed to coach her. *Let's come up with a goal—one goal!—for day one.*

The photo on her mirror was cut out from a magazine. It featured a woman with long, sometimes curly, blond hair. She was wearing a blue-and-gold glitter bodysuit and was holding a pale blue guitar. The background of the picture was dark, but phone lights shone around her like fireflies.

"One goal," Teffy said to herself. "Like make one friend?"

Yes! It felt as if the picture was smiling at her.

"I don't know," Teffy said worriedly, looking from the photo to her own reflection in the mirror. She still had a slight tan from the summer, and the tip of her nose was pink from last weekend's sunburn. (Her mom was always telling her to reapply her sunscreen. She vowed to do better.) But a sunburn wasn't the issue this morning. It was her hair. She'd parted her blond hair down the middle and made two French braids, but the right braid still looked lopsided. She was going for a look similar to Taylor's hair on the *evermore* album cover. French braiding was Teffy's super-power. Girls at her summer camp requested French braids all day long and doing hair had helped Teffy make friends. "I did meet Brooke, Audrey, and Scarlet doing braids, and when we talked, it turned out they liked lots of the same things I did."

See? the picture seemed to say.

She looked down at the multicolored beaded bracelets on her wrist. IN MY CAMP ERA said one. Audrey had made it for her. FRIEND4EVA was another. Scarlet had made one for each of them. "Why does middle school have to be so cruel?"

Hey. Cruel.

Teffy started to hum the bars to "Cruel Summer" as she finished tying the right braid again. Then she started riffing on the song's melody, creating her own lyrics for a new song.

"And it's new, my homeroom class is all new . . . and now I feel blue, and it's ooh, whoa, oh, it's a cruel homeroom. It's so cruel! No Audrey, Brooke, or Scarlet has left me feeling blue . . . Why can't I go to their school too? I don't want to be in Mr. Ball's class. Oooh! It's a cruel homeroom . . . without you."

Did her on-the-fly mixed-up song lyrics make sense? Not

exactly. But they calmed her down all the same. Writing lyrics was something Teffy loved doing, especially when she was anxious. Her secret dream was to someday write a song for Taylor.

Hey, a girl could dream.

Teffy's bedroom door opened and her brother, Charlie, poked his head inside. "Do I hear singing?" he asked with a lopsided grin.

"No. No singing," Teffy lied as she finished her braid and added a hair tie.

Charlie was three years older and entering eighth grade, which meant he was the king of the school. He opened the door wider, revealing his vintage tee, cargo shorts, and new white sneakers, which would be white for the next hour and then never again. (Charlie played football for the school's team, the Bulldogs, and their mom basically owned stock in bleach to keep his clothes clean.) Teffy had on new kicks too—white ones with a pale lavender stripe through the side like Scarlet and Audrey had on at camp. She was wearing a yellow floral sundress that felt like something Taylor would wear in her *folklore* era, so she was happy. She wanted to take a picture and show her dress to Scarlet, Audrey, and Brooke, but now that camp was over, she could only text them on her iPad.

Yep, she was the only fifth grader on the planet who didn't have a cell phone.

"Who are you talking to, Teffy?"

"I wasn't talking to anyone." She didn't trust Charlie with her secrets. Not after he told their friend and next-door neighbor Liam Yoon that she still slept with her closet light on.

Charlie stepped suspiciously into the room and his eyes went right to her bedroom vanity, where she kept her hair ties, bead kits, and her current favorite books. (Her mom liked to say she went through a book a day! Which was an exaggeration . . . sort of.) He pointed to the Taylor Swift photo taped to the glass on the vanity mirror.

Caught.

"You were talking to Taylor's picture again, weren't you?" Charlie held his stomach and laughed. "Weirdo! Mom said to get downstairs, or you'll miss the bus."

"I'm not a weirdo!" Teffy shouted, her face burning. "You're the weirdo for liking . . . um . . . the same band Grandpa likes. Who listens to the Rolling Stones?"

Charlie shook his head and kept laughing, not in the least bothered by her accusation. He slammed her door behind him.

Teffy looked at Taylor's picture again and sighed. "Is your brother as annoying as mine is?"

If talking to Taylor's photo about her biggest hopes, fears, and dreams was weird, she did not care. If anyone could understand what it was like to go through middle school, friend drama, boy drama, and everything and anything in between, it was Taylor Swift. And if Teffy wanted to be a songwriter even half as good as Taylor someday, then she needed to write in her journal and embrace her emotions.

She also had to find a way to get tickets to the Eras Tour.

Teffy glanced anxiously at her closet doors. She and her mom had painted them with pink magnetic chalkboard paint. The doors held family pictures, photos with friends, a list of books she'd read this year (she was closing in on a hundred thanks to summer camp), and a very large countdown chart. Today it said:

81 DAYS TILL THE ERAS TOUR.

Eighty-one days.

That's how long Teffy had to figure out a way to snag tickets to one of the concerts at Lucas Oil Stadium in Indianapolis. There were three nights she had a shot at. Three chances to see her absolute favorite singer-songwriter on the planet. She had to go. *Had to.* She knew the set list by heart, knew all about the "surprise" songs and outfit changes. She knew Taylor somehow made thousands of people in an arena feel like they were personal friends. Teffy wanted to be one of those friends so badly.

Teffy glanced at the picture on her mirror again and tried to manifest. "I'm going to make it happen. You watch. I'm going to get tickets to the Eras Tour."

"TEFFY! The bus!" her mom yelled again.

"Coming now!" Teffy turned back to the mirror. "But first, I need to survive day one of middle school. Wish me luck."

TWO
Change

There were five people standing at the bus stop when Teffy and Charlie made their way to the corner. They lived on a cul-de-sac with five houses, so everyone knew everyone at their bus stop. When Charlie ran ahead to talk to his friends, Teffy felt her stomach start to twist. *You're fine*, she reminded herself. *You can talk to Liam Yoon.*

Could a whole family be considered best friends? Teffy wasn't sure, but ever since the Yoons moved in four years ago, their families had become inseparable. Regular barbecues in one of their yards, camping trips every summer, and a standing date on New Year's Eve. If Teffy couldn't find her mom at home, the first thing she'd do was check the Yoons' front porch to see if her mom was there. The Yoon kids—Alex (who was Charlie's friend), Liam (who was one year older than Teffy and was her friend), and their younger sister, Jae (who was in third grade)—did the same thing when they couldn't find their own mom. Both moms took yoga classes together and went on long walks almost daily.

Maybe that's why Teffy wasn't surprised when their parents announced they were going into business together: Harrison by Design. The shop would print custom everything and anything for local teams and schools, from T-shirts to water bottles. Teffy's parents had wanted to open a store like this forever. The Yoons, who invested in a lot of businesses, had fronted them the money to finally open. Teffy couldn't wait to see her parents' dreams become reality when the store opened this spring.

"Hi, Liam," Teffy said, testing out this small talk thing. It was easier to do since it was Liam, but still. She had to start somewhere.

"Hey!" Liam walked over and stood beside her, adjusting his black backpack that was covered in patches from all the places the Yoons had been hiking over the years. "Ready for Harrison Middle?"

He was tall—as tall as Charlie, but not as tall as Alex—and Teffy liked how he usually always had on some variation of the same athletic tee with a small goat in the top right corner. (He told her the GOAT stood for "Greatest of All Time," which he said he was not, but it was something cool to strive for in football.)

"Not really," Teffy said, seeing Charlie talking to Alex and Kyle Fiero, another neighbor. The only other girls at the bus stop were Megan Tillmen and her twin sister, Rebecca, seventh graders who acted like Teffy didn't exist. "Charlie says when you know no one in your homeroom, you're doomed, but I'm going to try to make friends." *One friend. You can do this!* she pep-talked herself as she snuck a quick glance at her brother, who was laughing with his friends. How did he make it look so easy?

"Don't listen to him," Liam said, the light breeze blowing his floppy dark hair around. "I knew lots of people in homeroom last year, but my best friend? Matt? He was from Anderson Elementary, and I met him in homeroom. Now he and I are like this." He clasped his hands together. "You'll make friends."

"Thanks, Liam." Teffy grinned and her hand absentmindedly went to her hair.

Why was it always so easy to talk to Liam? She was never nervous around him. While Alex and Charlie liked to tease her and dunk her in the Yoons' pool, Liam had always been nice. Maybe it was because he was afraid she'd tell people he sang into his hairbrush too. She knew because their bedroom windows faced each other, and they were both averse to pulling down the shades till bedtime. Once she caught him singing and she started clapping. Liam looked embarrassed, then yelled, "Your turn!" She'd turned up "Lavender Haze" and belted it out. She liked to think they had a bond after that.

"I've got an idea," Liam said, his dark eyes glinting as the bus pulled up. "Maybe you'll be less nervous if you know your way around. I'll draw you a map on the bus so you don't get lost on your way to gym. It's in a hallway that I swear moves when no one is watching."

"That would be great." She laughed and followed him onto the bus. It was so packed, they would have had to sit together even if he hadn't asked. Teffy's stomach did a strange fluttering thing when she sat down next to Liam, their shoulders touching, but then she started to relax. By the time the bus rolled up to Harrison Middle, Teffy was feeling slightly better. Liam had told her where all the bathrooms were, which lunch line to get in if she wanted a shot at the deli counter, and how she was lucky to have her homeroom teacher, Mr. Ball. "He's the nicest, and he likes to do cool projects. Read and Rap, this group assignment, was my favorite," Liam said. "If you get the top score on a project or win a contest, he gives out Ball Bucks. They give you points on a test, a get-out-of-homework pass, and even gift cards to Ritter's for ice cream."

Gift cards to Ritter's? Teffy was sold.

"Go get 'em, Teffy!" Liam said, high-fiving her as they parted on the school's front steps and went in opposite directions.

That's when she felt a pit of dread form in her stomach again. She looked around at the groups of girls talking and tried to steady her breathing. *Today's goal is to make one friend. Not even a friend. Just talk to someone, Teffy. You can do this!*

Using Liam's map as a guide, Teffy found her way to the fifth-grade hallway in no time. She was halfway down the hall when a girl spun around fast and banged into her. Liam's cheat sheet went flying out of her hand.

"Gah! Sorry!" said the girl, first grabbing Teffy by the shoulders to steady her, then bending down to pick up the map. She was taller than Teffy by at least a foot. "Are you okay? Is this yours?"

"I'm fine and don't worry. I've got it," Teffy said, suddenly embarrassed for the girl to see Liam's map. She bent down fast too, and they almost crashed into each other again. The other girl laughed.

"Sorry. Again! I'm not usually such a klutz." She looked down at the paper in Teffy's hand and smiled. "Hey! I drew a map of the hallways too!" Her voice was loud, but she didn't seem the least bit embarrassed.

"You did?" Teffy said, surprised.

"Oh yeah." The girl whipped her own map out of a pocket in her skirt. She'd marked up the map with different colors and even had stick figures on it. "My dad and I came last week and walked all the halls to draw a map so I wouldn't get lost on the way to my locker."

She had a bright smile, brown eyes, and springy coils that bounced when she moved, which was a lot as she gestured with her hands. She was giving off Halle Bailey vibes. Her nails were painted bright blue and she had double ear piercings with star earrings—one pair pink, one pair blue. The girl was wearing a pink tee that said STRONG LIKE A GIRL and a swishy black athletic skirt with shorts peeking out underneath. She had the same sneakers Teffy did.

"But I guess we didn't do a great job," the girl continued, trying to view her own map from every angle. "Because I am still lost."

Teffy took a deep breath. "I think I know where I'm going. Want me to help you?"

The girl's eyes lit up. "Really? That would be great. Thanks!" she said enthusiastically.

"No problem," Teffy said, and her stomach unclenched. "Where are you trying to go?"

"I'm looking for 22B. Mr. Ball's class. He's a fifth-grade teacher."

Teffy's heart leapt. "I have Mr. Ball too!"

"You do?" The other girl squealed, throwing her arms around Teffy as if they were long-lost friends. "This is so great! I'm Taylor, by the way. My dad is a Swiftie and named me after Taylor, which is awesome because I love her more than I love PB and J."

"That's my name too," said Teffy, getting goose bumps. What were the odds? "And my parents named me after Taylor too. We're huge fans."

Taylor squealed again. "No. Way!"

The two girls looked at each other in awe.

Taylor linked her arm through Teffy's. "It's official. We're meant to be friends."

Teffy felt her face beam. *Friends. I did it. And school hasn't even started yet.*

Suddenly, entering Mr. Ball's homeroom didn't seem so scary.

"I think so too. Follow me," Teffy said, leading the way. "I know where we need to go."

THREE

Karma

By the time the Taylors found Mr. Ball's classroom, Teffy learned that the other Taylor, Taylor Johnson, went by Tay Tay and had recently moved to Indianapolis by way of Naples, Florida. Her new home was only a few blocks away from Teffy's. Teffy knew exactly where Tay Tay's house was because it was right next to Sweet Greens Christmas Tree Farm. ("Again, fate!" Tay Tay said emphatically, waving wildly. "First, I get a Christmas tree farm for a backyard, and then I'm sent another Taylor. I'm liking Indianapolis already.")

Tay Tay said she was an only child who had been raised by her dad since she was a baby, and her favorite thing in the whole world was gymnastics. She'd done it four days a week in Florida, "but now I want to try something new," Tay Tay told her. "I wonder if there is such a thing as singing gymnastics." Her eyes widened. "A floor routine to a Taylor song would be amazing."

Teffy laughed. She liked how Tay Tay filled up all the available silences between them. Sometimes Tay Tay didn't even come up for air between sentences. Teffy was not a big talker unless she knew someone really well, and when she was nervous? Like she'd been this morning? She tended to be even quieter than normal. But Tay Tay put her so at ease that she shared her nickname, and Tay Tay recognized the reference immediately. "You look like a Teffy," she insisted.

"Okay, favorite Taylor song?" Tay Tay asked.

"Easy! It's still 'Style,'" Teffy told her. "Unless we're talking new stuff from *The Tortured Poets Department*, then it's 'I Can Do It with a Broken Heart.'"

Tay Tay nodded. "I love that song. I also love 'Down Bad.'"

"Me too!"

"But my all-time favorite Taylor song?" Tay Tay thought for a moment. "I don't know. I can't pick. But I love 'Getaway Car.'"

"Me too!" Teffy said again, and they grinned at each other.

That's when Teffy realized they were in front of classroom 22B. *Oh my my my.*

"This is Mr. Ball's room," Teffy said, her voice getting quiet again.

Tay Tay looked at the number on the door and yanked Teffy inside. "Let's go fight dragons together. We can sit next to each other until Mr. Ball realizes I talk too much and moves me away from you."

Teffy liked Tay Tay's idea, but entering Mr. Ball's room, Teffy felt a slight flutter ripple through her stomach, like a wave. This was it. Homeroom. Even with Tay Tay beside her, she was still nervous, but a quick look around told her the classroom didn't look that different from the ones at Old Mill Elementary. There were the same colorful charts about grammar nestled between inspirational posters that said things like: YOU'VE GOT THIS . . . AND MORE. Mr. Ball seemed to like travel because there were also posters of countries all over the world and numerous pictures of London with Mr. Ball in them.

Their new teacher was at his desk, typing something on his computer. Short and stocky with dark hair, pale skin, and glasses, he also had pictures behind him on a bulletin board of a cute bulldog and what Teffy assumed was his family—two dark-haired little girls and a wife. In one photo they were on vacation standing in front of a castle! Cool.

"Sit here," Tay Tay whispered, pointing to a desk in the middle of the room, three rows from the front but not all the way in the back, where it felt like all the boys were seated, talking loud and laughing. Teffy took a seat. Tay Tay sat across from her and crossed her fingers. "Here's to a good year!" she said louder than necessary, but it was hard to ignore her enthusiasm.

Teffy crossed her fingers too and repeated the words in her head. *Here's to a good year! And Mr. Ball not moving Tay Tay's seat!*

The bell rang and Mr. Ball stood up. "Morning, class!" The room quieted, except for some continued whispering in the back row. "I, as you may have guessed, am Mr. Ball, your fearless leader aka homeroom teacher as well as your travel agent, personal calculator, and guide to the stars, as science is my specialty subject." He smiled. "Welcome to fifth grade!" There was some nervous laughter, and Teffy and Tay Tay looked at each other. "Quiet group, huh? You weren't so quiet a few minutes ago." He picked up a clipboard. There was a picture of the Leaning Tower of Pisa on the back. "Let's see who we've got on our team this year. When I call your name, please raise your hand and say 'here.'"

Teffy sat up straighter. As someone with a *B* last name, she knew she could be called any minute, and she was, right after Rahul Ahuja.

"Taylor Bennett?" Mr. Ball called.

Teffy raised her hand and he nodded at her. Then she sat back to relax for the next few minutes, zoning out and organizing her new glitter pencils in rainbow-color order in her pencil box while she waited for Tay Tay's name to be called.

"Two Taylors?" questioned a kid in the back row.

"Try *four* Taylors," said Mr. Ball, and Teffy and Tay Tay looked at each other in surprise. "Where are Taylor Perez and Taylor Shaw?"

Two girls on opposite sides of the classroom raised their hands. The girl to her right Teffy recognized from summer camp. Taylor Perez had long, raven-colored hair tied back in a cute bun, light brown skin, and was wearing a black romper with glittery high-tops that showed off her tall and slender frame. She had over a dozen friendship bracelets on her wrists. Teffy wasn't surprised. Taylor P. was one of the most popular girls at camp. They weren't in the same cabin, so they'd never spoken before, but Teffy had seen Taylor P. in action. She seemed sort of bossy at camp, but in a good way. If someone was being picked on at camp, she'd step in. If the fruit choices at lunch were lacking, or her bunk didn't want to spend the afternoon fencing, Taylor P. was the one most vocal about it.

The other Taylor—Taylor Shaw—had distinct long red hair with loose curls. Her hair was so long it reached the center of her back in a ponytail. She was tall, like Tay Tay, with pale skin marked with sunburn splotches on her arms. On her left arm, Teffy noticed a faint temporary tattoo of a soccer ball. Taylor S. had also Sharpie'd words on her right arm that had since smudged, making them impossible to read. She was wearing a pink Messi jersey with a black skort.

"Four Taylors might be a new personal record of Taylors I've had in class," Mr. Ball told them. "Not to worry. We'll manage." He looked at each of them and scratched his chin. "I think the best thing to do for now is go by first name, last initial. Unless any of you go by a nickname you want to use instead?"

Teffy looked around. Did she speak up and share her nickname? She felt a tightness in her chest at the thought of raising her hand and speaking up. Was "Teffy" babyish or cool? She waited for Tay Tay to speak first, but when her new friend didn't offer up her nickname either, Teffy stayed silent.

"First name, last initial it is!" Mr. Ball said.

Teffy had never been with another Taylor in class before, but she knew Brooke from camp dealt with this, as her name was so popular. There were upsides and downsides to being one of four Taylors in a classroom, as far as Teffy could tell. If someone said "Taylor?" everyone was going to turn around. But the upside was that if Mr. Ball called on her and she didn't know the answer, there was a good chance she could pretend to think he called on someone else.

"Four Taylors?" One of the boys in the back spoke up again. "Why would anyone name a girl Taylor? It's a boy's name." A few kids laughed and Teffy found herself suddenly fascinated with the heart-shaped eraser she'd placed on her desk.

A chair screeched. Teffy looked up and saw Taylor P. stand. "Who wouldn't want to be named after the greatest singer-songwriter of all time? Taylor Alison Swift?"

Teffy and Tay Tay looked at each other and smiled. Another Swiftie? Before Teffy could even react, she saw Taylor S. jump up from her side of the room and give a loud cheer. "Let's hear it for the Taylor Swift Fan Club!"

All four Taylors were Swifties?

She looked at Tay Tay. She was sure her new friend would call it karma. The lyrics to the song started playing in her head.

Tay Tay stood up fast, applauding too.

The class was riled up now—some kids booing (*the haters gonna hate, hate, hate*), but more kids were cheering, the volume in the class growing louder. Mr. Ball just grinned, looking amused at the reaction.

All three Taylors, now standing tall, looked over at Teffy expectantly.

And that's when Teffy realized something—whether she was shy about speaking up or not, whether the four of them knew one another or not, they were connected. They were a team of Taylor Swift–loving Taylors.

And that was one thing Teffy could definitely get behind.

Teffy pushed her chair out and rose up with pride. The other three Taylors cheered even louder.

Maybe, Teffy thought, middle school wouldn't be so bad after all.

FOUR

This Is Why We Can't Have Nice Things

Teffy had to admit: The first week of fifth grade wasn't that bad. Mr. Ball didn't give any homework. Instead, they had to have their parents sign forms about codes of conduct and borrowing technology, and—in what Teffy thought was the best assignment ever—each student had to decorate their writer's notebook with inspirational photos, stickers, and quotes. Teffy's notebook was stickered both front and back with pictures of Taylor in concert, with her guitar and without, and with her dancers and friends. Teffy used whatever she could find online that she could print without using too much of the family's color ink in the printer.

Mr. Ball, Teffy learned on the bus from Liam, was "super into writing." And that, Teffy thought, was great because she planned on filling her writer's notebook up with all sorts of inspiring stories and maybe even some song lyrics.

Teffy had already promised the Taylor picture on her mirror that this would be the year she wrote actual songs and pushed herself to be braver. Talk to people, not wait for someone to talk to her first. Do things, like actually join an after-school club or activity. She'd been in the same dance class since she was seven, mostly because she was always too afraid to try something new, but it was time she gave new activities a chance. She'd already completed her first goal and made one friend—hadn't she?

Could she call Tay Tay her friend for real? They hadn't hung out after school yet, but Tay Tay had asked for Teffy's phone number. Teffy was embarrassed when she had to give her email address instead, but Tay Tay hadn't said anything about it. They'd messaged a few times, mostly memes and Taylor stuff. They talked every day in school, and Tay Tay's exuberance was hard to ignore. It made Teffy want to speak up, even if she was nervous.

When Teffy got to school on Monday, she found Tay Tay waiting by their lockers. "Hey!" she shouted so loud that everyone in the hallway turned to look. Tay Tay didn't care. "Look at my writer's notebook!" Tay Tay held it up and waved it in the air like a pom-pom. This week, her nails were painted lavender.

"I used all Eras Tour photos, but the back is all photos from the Red Tour, since *Red—Taylor's Version*, of course—is one of my favorite albums."

"Every album is your favorite," Teffy teased, feeling comfortable enough around Tay Tay to joke with her now. "Mine too."

"Twins!" Tay Tay beamed. "Can I see your notebook?"

"Sure." Teffy sat down and pulled her almost unrecognizable marble notebook out of her shiny pink backpack. She handed it to Tay Tay.

She examined Teffy's notebook from all sides. "This came out so good. Did you laminate it?"

"My mom used clear packing tape because chances are, I will spill something on this book at some point this year," Teffy admitted, and Tay Tay laughed.

"I probably will too. I need to tell my dad to buy tape." Tay Tay examined each photo closely. "I love how we both used the same photo of Taylor in the red glitter outfit with red booties. We really are twins." The first bell rang. "Come on." Tay Tay jumped up and pulled Teffy with her. "Let's see if we can make it a second week without Mr. Ball changing our seats!"

—•~•-T-A-y-L-O-R-S-•~•—

They made it through the morning sitting side by side, but Teffy suspected their days were numbered. Mr. Ball noticed Tay Tay whispering a lot. Teffy was dreading a seat change. At least she had Tay Tay with her at lunch. She didn't think she'd survive the lunch table otherwise. The lunch aides had assigned their tables, like they were in kindergarten! Teffy and Tay Tay had to sit with Hannah Reed and Greta Lucca, two of the least friendly girls in class. After Hannah made a comment about Teffy's lunch bag, Teffy knew she and Hannah would never be friends. Her bag was teal and not a name brand, which apparently made it "fake." Teffy wasn't sure how Tay Tay felt about the girls. She didn't want to be rude and ask.

When the bell rang for the lunch period, Teffy felt a knot start to form in her stomach. She'd promised herself she'd be brave and talk more, but with Hannah and Greta commanding the table, she clammed up more than ever. Not Tay Tay.

"Who wants to share some of my chocolate pretzels?" Tay Tay asked, pulling a bag of pretzel rods covered in chocolate and sprinkles out of her lunch sack, which was plain purple. Teffy was sure Hannah hated it too. "My dad bought them at the Sweet Greens gift shop over the weekend and they're so good."

"I'll have one. Also, the Christmas tree farm is open in August?" Teffy asked, sitting down beside her. The other girls at the table were busy getting out their lunches and talking amongst themselves. The center seats at the table remained empty.

"They have a Christmas-themed coffee shop year-round," Tay Tay said, bouncing up and down in her seat. "And, ooh! Ooh! They have hot chocolate—actual hot chocolate *and* the frozen kind. You have to come over to my house and we can go try it."

A hangout? Yes! "Okay," Teffy said happily.

And then Hannah sat down in the middle of the table.

"I love your shirt," Tatjana Sanchez said to Hannah. It was a fitted white tee with a black-and-white sketch of a city, boats drifting through the water in front of a pretty street. In blue bubble letters at the top was a brand and the city name: AMSTERDAM.

"I got it when I was on vacation there this summer. Where did everyone else go?" Hannah asked the table, commanding the conversation before people could even unwrap their sandwiches.

Everyone looked at one another nervously. Teffy deflated and grew quiet. They'd been camping with the Yoons, but with her parents getting ready to open Harrison by Design, money was tight.

Tay Tay looked around and shrugged. "Does moving from Florida to Indianapolis count as a vacation?"

"No," Hannah said decisively. "Anyone else?"

"We went to Cedar Point amusement park in Ohio," Greta told the group. "The park has so many good coasters, but the five-hour car ride was bad." She took a sip from her pricey water bottle (she and Hannah had matching pink ones). "My brother threw up twice."

Two other girls spoke up—one had visited her grandmother's house in Michigan and another had gone to New York City, which sounded amazing, but Hannah waited till everyone had spoken to drop her bombshell.

"Want to know why I was in Amsterdam?" Hannah asked, smiling triumphantly. "I was seeing Taylor Swift."

Teffy almost dropped her peanut butter sandwich in her lap. She'd noticed Hannah wearing an Eras Tour shirt last week, but it felt like a lot of fifth graders had tour shirts, whether they'd gone to see Taylor in another city already or not. Teffy glanced sideways at Tay Tay as if to say, *Wow*.

"You saw the Eras concert in Amsterdam?" Jana Masdern gripped her orange lunch box.

"Yes. My parents said I could pick any city I wanted to see her in, and anyone can go to New York. I wanted to go to Amsterdam. So we went," Hannah said, practically smirking as she pulled another item out of her lunch bag, which was just a popular athletic brand's store bag. It seemed like several girls used the store bag as a lunch tote too.

Teffy's mom refused to pay a hundred dollars for a pair of leggings. So obviously, Teffy did not have a bag from that store. She didn't have the pricey water bottle that Greta and Hannah had either.

"Wow," said Lanie Chu, the chocolate-covered pretzel rod from Tay Tay in her right hand frozen in mid-air. "You're so lucky." She looked around at the table. "I know a girl at my summer camp whose mom paid almost ten thousand dollars a ticket. They're seeing Taylor in Vancouver."

"Ten thousand a ticket?" Tay Tay scoffed. "Tickets don't cost that much, do they?"

"They could," said Greta, and looked at Hannah. "Did yours?"

"I don't know," Hannah said, munching on baby carrots. "All I know is that I'm going to see her again at Lucas Oil Stadium for the Saturday show."

At this, Teffy did drop something—her mini bag of chips. Half of them scattered across the floor. Hannah noticed.

"How'd you get tickets?" Jana asked, her voice a reverent whisper. "Not through the presale, right? Because no one I know got them."

"My neighbor did," Teffy spoke up, trying hard to recover from the Potato Chip Incident. "She had a preorder code and she said she logged in that morning and got right in the queue. She bought six tickets for around a hundred dollars each."

Hearing Mrs. Yoon talk about getting tickets felt like hearing someone say they saw an actual unicorn. But it was true—Mrs. Yoon got tickets for herself, Jae, and four cousins. Teffy's mom had a code too (their whole extended family signed up for codes to try to get them a better chance), but she didn't have the same luck. Mrs. Yoon had felt bad Teffy didn't get seats.

"I have floor seats," Hannah said triumphantly, "and"—she looked around at the table—"my dad said my sister and I can each pick a friend to go with us to the show."

Teffy and Tay Tay glanced at each other. Teffy hoped Tay Tay was thinking the same thing: that if there was one reason to say no to an Eras Tour ticket, it was going with Hannah.

Greta turned her whole body sideways to face Hannah. "Did you, um, pick anyone yet?"

Hannah became very interested in putting the small butterfly-shaped cap on her water bottle's straw. "Nope. I'm trying to decide who I really want to see the show with." She looked pointedly at Greta. "I only want a *real* fan going. You still don't know all the lyrics to 'Lover.'"

"That's not true!" Greta squeaked. "I know them! I just get tripped up on the chorus."

Hannah eyed her with skepticism, pushing her wavy brown hair away from her face again. "I heard you singing on the bus this morning. You forgot the words to half the song. A true fan knows all the lyrics to all the songs."

Greta looked down, her face red. Teffy thought she saw tears prick the corners of Greta's eyes. Teffy felt bad for her. No one knew the lyrics to *every* Taylor song, did they? She knew the lyrics to her favorite songs, yes, but not every single one. She wished she could tell Greta that, but Teffy did not want to cross Hannah. It didn't seem like anyone else wanted to either.

A few girls talked about their parents trying to get tickets on resale sites. Jana said her dad's sister's best friend's cousin might possibly maybe know someone at Taylor Swift's label that could get her tickets. Jessica Pierce, who had a strawberry-shaped lunch bag, heard that a satellite radio station called Taylor's Era was giving away tickets every weekend until the tour came to town.

Tay Tay turned to Teffy. "My dad's job has a box at Lucas Oil so he said he'd try to get tickets, but it's not looking good. We tried for the Tampa show and couldn't get those either. My dad said no concert should cost more than three hundred dollars a ticket, and even that's a stretch." She sighed heavily and fiddled with a rope bracelet on her wrist. "I haven't seen anything online for under five hundred dollars so I'm thinking about giving up hope."

"My mom can't spend more than a hundred," Teffy said, and Tay Tay winced. "I know that's not a lot. Other than my neighbor, I don't know anyone who got tickets that cheap. I told my mom I'd chip in my birthday money, but it's not going to be enough. I've made a list of ways to try to find cheap tickets though." Teffy pulled out her notebook and showed it to Tay Tay.

Tay Tay brightened. "Tell me more!"

Teffy shook her head. "I read on a fan page that sometimes you can get last-minute tickets using a hashtag on social media with the show date, but my mom thinks we'll be scammed. So I'm trying to raise money to afford tickets. Last weekend I washed both cars, and our neighbors' cars, and did weeding." She made a face. "I made thirty dollars."

Tay Tay bit her lip. "This plan of yours could take till Taylor's next tour." Teffy deflated till Tay Tay hit her arm and said, "But hey! What if we teamed up? If we both raise money, maybe we will have enough for nosebleed seats."

Teffy brightened. "Yes! That's a great idea."

Tay Tay bounced up and down on the bench. "This could work."

"It could," Teffy said, feeling better already. Maybe together they had a chance. And a chance was all they needed.

"Stop worrying, girls!" she overheard Hannah tell the lunch table. "The concert isn't for another two months. You all still have time to impress me."

Teffy and Tay Tay shared a grin. Who needed Hannah? They had each other.

FIVE

Shake It Off

By the end of the second week of middle school, Teffy felt like a pro. Walk to the back of the bus and find a seat in the morning? Easy. Navigate a packed hallway to get to the fifth-grade wing? No problem. Her homework was up-to-date for the week (she'd used colored highlighters to check off each and every assignment) and she was looking forward to the weekend. That Friday morning she'd even decided maybe *she'd* be brave enough to be the one to ask Tay Tay to make plans to hang out.

But the morning took a dark turn.

Teffy had just reached her locker (which she'd decorated with a mini mirror, camp photos, and one of Taylor, naturally) when Greta approached her.

"Hey," said Greta, hugging her writer's notebook to her chest. The front of her notebook had a massive picture of a giant black sheepdog. A few stickers from restaurants and one of a beach umbrella surrounded him. At the bottom was a tiny photo of Greta with Hannah.

"Hey," Teffy said back because she wasn't sure what to say other than *You're blocking me from opening my locker*. Plus, Greta never spoke to her unless it was at the lunch table and only after Hannah spoke to Teffy first. Which wasn't often.

Greta's brown eyes seemed to widen as she spoke. "So I don't want to sound mean because it's not you, but you need to switch to the other girls' lunch table today. And stay there," she added as an afterthought.

"Why?" Teffy asked quietly. Because she didn't know what to say. She just started picking at her chipped pink nail polish absentmindedly, which was something she did when she was nervous. *Did I do something wrong?* she wanted to ask but didn't.

"Hannah just found out she's allergic to peanuts and you and Taylor J. are always bringing peanut butter to lunch. And it's dangerous for Hannah so Claire Maguire and Allison Yang are going to switch with you two. Okay? Thanks!" She didn't wait for Teffy to reply. She just smiled thinly and turned around. Teffy watched as Greta speed walked over to Hannah, who was waiting by her own locker. The two started whispering and Teffy saw Hannah look her way.

Teffy avoided eye contact. Peanut butter? "But I haven't had that since the first day of school," Teffy said under her breath. This was just an excuse to vote them off the lunch table. Tears pricked the corners of Teffy's eyes. She barely spoke at lunch. What had she or Tay Tay done wrong? She wasn't overly fond of Hannah or Greta, but being kicked off the lunch table was still harsh. Was that even allowed?

"Happy Fri-YAY!" Tay Tay shouted, and did a jump in the air for good measure as she came up from behind her. Her teal backpack was slung over one arm and she was wearing an athletic skirt and a tank top that said BE KIND. "Guess what? I made fifteen dollars last night taking all our recycling to the supermarket. More money for our tickets! Yay!" She saw Teffy's face and frowned. "What's wrong?"

"Greta just voted you and me off the lunch table. She said Claire and Allison are taking our seats and we have to go to the other lunch table to sit. For the rest of the year," Teffy added, trying not to sound upset.

Tay Tay bear-hugged her. "Thank the fairies! We've been saved!"

Teffy blinked "Wait. You're okay with this?"

"Aren't you? This is the best news ever!" Tay Tay let go and did a few dance moves, not caring who was looking at her in the hallway. When she saw Teffy's stunned face, she stopped. "Aren't you happy? That table had bad energy. I've been telling the fairies that live in the trees at the Christmas tree farm that we need their magic to deal with the Hannahs and the Gretas of fifth grade, and look! We've been moved!"

"You talk to fairies?" Teffy tried not to laugh. "At Sweet Greens?"

Tay Tay nodded solemnly. "My dad and I take walks there at night on the farm—Steve, the owner, doesn't mind—and so many trees have these adorable hand-painted fairy doors, so I thought to myself, if there is a door, then there must be a fairy." She shrugged. "It doesn't hurt to believe, does it?" She grinned. "It worked in our favor!"

Teffy slowly smiled. Tay Tay was right. This was good news. No more dreading the lunch table. "Thank the fairies, then! Lunch table two, here we come!"

Literally, "here we come," because right after free writing time and math, and before Mr. Ball taught them about butterfly metamorphosis (something they'd be witnessing when they hatched butterflies this spring), Teffy found herself following Tay Tay to their new table.

"Hi!" Tay Tay said to the table with spirit. "We're your new lunch mates!"

Kim Cohen looked up from her salad, which was in a bento box with a cute star-shaped sandwich, bear cookies, and grapes, and smiled. "Welcome to table two!"

The other girls smiled too. Not fake smiles. Genuine ones. Beth Monir even scooched down so Teffy would have more room. Teffy felt her stomach unclench. Maybe this lunch table would be better after all.

Teffy and Tay Tay took seats at one end across from each other. Ironically, they were seated next to Taylor P. and Taylor S. on either side of the table.

"Hey," said Taylor S. with a sympathetic smile. Her long red hair was knotted on top of her head, allowing Teffy to clearly see she was wearing tiny silver soccer ball cleats as earrings. Written in blue was the number 8. She had to assume that was Taylor S.'s jersey number. Today she was wearing another soccer jersey. "We heard what happened with Greta. I'm sorry. She's basically

Hannah's minion." Taylor S. took a bite of a peanut butter and jelly sandwich. *How ironic!* Teffy thought. "And I don't mean the cute little yellow guys. I mean she's like Hannah's henchman."

Teffy and Tay Tay laughed. Taylor S. seemed nice.

"This isn't funny," Taylor P. snapped, and everyone at the lunch table seemed to stop what they were doing when they heard her voice. Taylor P., from what Teffy knew from watching her at a distance during camp, could command a room with a single sentence. "Where do Hannah and Greta get off telling people where to sit in the lunchroom? Do they work for Harrison Middle School now?" A few girls laughed nervously.

"Oh boy," Taylor S. said under her breath.

Teffy's jaw dropped in horror as she watched Taylor P. stand up and point to Hannah and Greta across the lunchroom. "Hannah is a coward. And I'd be happy to say that to their faces!"

SIX

Speak Now

"Sit down!" Taylor S. pulled Taylor P. back to the bench before Hannah, Greta, or a lunch aide saw what was going on. "Are you trying to start a fight and get detention?"

"Oh pul-eeze," Taylor P. said with an eye roll. "They didn't even hear me." She bit into her apple and Teffy watched as the little glitter star tattoo on her cheek moved up and down as she chewed. It matched the glitter on her shirt and her high-top sneakers. It even matched the clip in her long, dark hair. "I just hate mean girls."

Me too, Teffy thought, in awe of Taylor P.'s boldness. She loved how Taylor P. wasn't afraid of anyone. Even Hannah.

"Still!" Taylor S. scolded. "There is no need to start a lunchroom war, is there? It's the second week of school."

"No, lunch wars do not sound fun," Tay Tay agreed, and held up a pretzel. "Though I have always wanted to be in a food fight."

"Me too!" Taylor S. gushed, and they smiled at each other. She unzipped a lunch box with a cat picture on it. Inside was a water bottle with preschool show characters on it. Teffy had noticed Taylor S.'s writer's notebook was as unique as she was—sports pics, cat stickers, cartoon characters saying cheesy lines, and a photo of a homemade donut. "My point is, let's all relax." She looked at Teffy and Tay Tay. "The truth is, we'd rather sit with you two. And I'm sure you two would rather sit with us. This lunch switcheroo is a good thing and if there is a lunchroom table competition, now we will win hands down!"

"Okay, Coach TS," Taylor P. said, cracking a small smile. "My rant is over."

"Sorry." Taylor S. looked sheepishly at Teffy, her nose scrunching up tight, showing off all her freckles. "I can be a little competitive."

Taylor P. raised her right eyebrow. "A little, TS? Yesterday you made everyone at the table vote on who had the best snack at lunch when you brought in your homemade trail mix that everyone is obsessed with."

"It's all about the seasonings," TS said with confidence.

"Of course," Tay Tay agreed. "I even put everything bagel seasoning on my pizza!"

"Me too!" Taylor S. grinned. "TS is my nickname, by the way. You might think it's cheesy, but I love it. You can call me that too if you want. It's what they call me at soccer." She thought for a moment. "And volleyball. And on winter track. I'm captain of all three travel teams."

"Wow, you do a lot," Teffy marveled.

"I only do gymnastics, but I haven't signed up for a gym here yet," Tay Tay said. "I heard there's a cheerleading meeting after school today, so I thought I'd go."

"TS and I are going to that too," Taylor P said. "Are you both going to try out?"

"Well, I'm hoping I can squeeze it in," TS said, munching on a carrot stick. Her right arm had multiple friendship bracelets on it, just like Teffy's. "Soccer practice isn't till six and cheerleading is right after school so I might be able to swing both. *If* I make the team."

"We can all go together," said Tay Tay, and she looked at Teffy. "You should come too. Didn't you say you take dance class at the rec center?"

"Yes, but . . ." Teffy hedged. It was one thing to take a dance class. It was another to want to be a cheerleader—which was everything she wasn't. Bold. Loud. Outgoing.

Try new things, she told herself again. *Be brave.*

"My sister would kill me if I didn't try out," said Taylor P. She had on mascara and lip gloss. Her nails were painted baby blue, like Tay Tay's, and her ears were pierced. Her whole vibe was impossibly cool. "She started cheering for the Bulldogs when she was my age and all three of my brothers play football. My parents have been to more open houses at Harrison MS than Principal Moody. I'm the last one," she added, stirring the pesto pasta in her aluminum container. "Which means Mr. Ball can compare me to all four of my siblings. *Fun.*"

Teffy was surprised to hear her say that. She assumed Taylor P. would have an easy time at Harrison Middle. *Maybe*, Teffy thought, *starting middle school is hard for everyone.*

"How do you two like Mr. Ball?" TS asked Teffy. "My brother and sister had him, so I figured I was getting him, and I'm glad. He's sooo nice, and I love Indy Trivia. I'm determined to get the high score for the year."

TS really was competitive. "I like Indy Trivia too," said Teffy, speaking up finally.

Indy Trivia was an Indianapolis trivia game that Mr. Ball played sometimes between subjects. He split the classroom in two teams—down the middle—and the winning team got to pick prizes from his prize box or rack up points that could be used for pizza parties, a movie break, or extra time outside.

"I like how Mr. Ball runs it like a game show," Tay Tay added. "He's got a great announcer voice."

"He needs a new game already," Taylor P. cut in. "All four of my siblings had Mr. Ball before me and he does the same trivia every. Single. Year. I pretty much know all the answers already. I should tell him that."

Tay Tay cleared her throat. "Taylor P., I just wanted to say, I loved how you stuck up for Taylors everywhere and Swifties the first day of school."

Taylor P. groaned. "Thanks, but do you really have to call me Taylor P.? It sounds so weird. Doesn't it?" She looked at TS. "It's like we're in a girl group or something." They all laughed. "I can't do all year as a Taylor P. I am Taylor. My name is the one thing I have that's really mine and I don't want to be called by anything else."

"What do you mean?" Tay Tay asked.

Taylor P. shifted uncomfortably on the lunch bench. "I'm the youngest of five, which means I'm the last for everything." For once, Taylor P. sounded small. "Last one in the car, last one to get new stuff. I get all the hand-me-downs—sports equipment, bedroom furniture, all my sister's old clothes. And it's fine. I get we don't have the money to do it all, but I don't want to share my name." Her face colored. "I guess what I'm trying to say is, I don't want to be called 'Taylor P.' I just want to be called 'Taylor.'" She looked around the crowded lunchroom. "Harrison has been so hard already. All my friends went to the other middle school in the district, and I knew no one in our homeroom class when we got here. My name is all I've got." She looked down at her lunch box. "I don't know if that sounds silly, but . . ."

Teffy couldn't believe it. Taylor P. seemed so confident and sure of herself. It made Teffy remember, no one really knows what is going on in someone else's head. She was glad Taylor P. spoke up. "It makes a lot of sense," Teffy said gently. "You should get to be our class's 'Taylor.'"

Taylor P. smiled unsurely. "Yeah?"

They all nodded.

"I go by Tay Tay anyway," Tay Tay told her.

"And my family calls me Teffy," said Teffy, feeling silly.

Taylor grinned. "Isn't that what Taylor Swift's brother calls her?" Teffy nodded. "Cool! I like it. *Teffy*." They smiled at each other.

"Me too," agreed TS. She held up a carrot stick like a sword. "So it's settled—from here forth, let it be known that the Taylors of Mr. Ball's room are Taylor, TS, Tay Tay, and Teffy."

The Taylors. Teffy liked that.

Taylor laughed. "You really are cheesy."

"I'm proud of my cheesiness!" TS looked around at Teffy and Tay Tay. "There's only one thing left to ask: Are you two also named after *the* Taylor?"

Teffy and Tay Tay nodded.

"I knew it!" TS held out her arm. "I just got goose bumps."

"Me too," said Teffy, starting to feel more comfortable. She'd never met other girls named after Taylor like she was.

"My sister is the oldest and she was the one who won baby-naming rights for the youngest—surprise!—baby in the family," Taylor told them. "She's a Swiftie too, and before you ask, my favorite song is 'New Romantics,' my favorite album is *1989*, and no, I'm not going to the concert because, unlike Hannah, my family can't afford five-thousand-dollar tickets."

"Five thousand dollars?" Tay Tay gaped.

"That's what we heard she was paying for floor seats, but Hannah could be lying," TS said. "We couldn't get tickets either. Are either of you going to one of the concerts when she comes to town?"

Teffy and Tay Tay shook their heads.

"Teffy and I made a pact to try to raise money to buy tickets together on a resale site," Tay Tay told them.

Taylor's eyebrows shot up. "How much do you have so far?"

Teffy grimaced. "About three hundred dollars."

Taylor's frown deepened. "I don't think that's enough to even find one ticket, but who knows? My mom had a friend get tickets at face value from another friend who scored better seats. So maybe it can happen."

"Five thousand dollars a ticket," Tay Tay repeated, and looked at Teffy. "If that's what it would cost to see the show, we are doomed."

Teffy felt the pit in her stomach grow again. Was getting tickets that impossible?

TS placed her hands on the table with a loud thump. "Enough feeling sorry for ourselves! We may not have Taylor tickets, but what we do have is this awesome new Taylor group."

"So we're a group?" Taylor teased.

"Yes, a lunch group, at least, and I think we could also be the Taylor . . . cheerleaders!" Her eyes gleamed mischievously. "Come on, we should all try out together. Wouldn't that be fun?"

Teffy suddenly realized all the girls were looking at her.

"Am I really the only one not trying out?" Teffy asked, trying not to sound nervous.

"Yep! You're the holdout," said Taylor, who stared at Teffy curiously. "Hey. I just realized why you look so familiar. You went to Red Pines Summer Camp this summer, didn't you?"

Speak, Teffy. Speak! "Yeah. I thought you looked familiar too." *Why didn't I say something sooner?*

Taylor's eyes lit up. "Yes, you're the girl who wrote that really funny camp song that the other girls' bunk performed at the talent show, aren't you?"

The other Taylors all looked at her anew.

Teffy's face grew hot. "Guilty."

"Guilty?" Taylor threw a potato chip at her. "That song was so funny, my bunk was singing it for days."

"That's so cool!" Tay Tay nudged her. "You didn't tell me you wrote songs."

"Just for fun . . . for now," Teffy said, embarrassed.

"You're good," said Taylor and she sounded honest. "You should have performed it too. And you should definitely come to the cheer meeting. My sister said they're always looking for new cheers. You could write them."

"I don't like getting up in front of people," Teffy admitted, picking at her nails again. "It makes me nervous."

"We'll be with you the whole time." TS gave Teffy's hand a squeeze. "It would be fun if all the Taylors were cheerleaders together."

It did sound fun. And scary. And fun. She looked around at the other girls.

Together. Maybe cheer tryouts wouldn't be so scary if she had the other Taylors with her. "Okay," Teffy said, gaining courage. "I'm in."

SEVEN

Look What You Made Me Do

It felt like every girl in middle school was at the cheer meeting.

The gym was hot, sweaty, and packed when the four Taylors arrived right after the last bell rang. Teffy was so nervous she tried counting heads but lost track. She spotted several familiar faces from Mr. Ball's class, including Hannah and Greta, who were sitting with a few girls from her *former* lunch table. *Whatever*, she told herself. Her new lunch table was much better already. She didn't feel too sick to eat after listening to everyone around her talk. And all four of the Taylors were with her here now. That made her feel good.

"There's so many people here," said Tay Tay, running a hand over her curls, which she'd tied back with a red headband. "I wonder how many girls they're taking for the squad."

"My sister said they never have more than thirty girls per squad," Taylor told her as she started to stretch her legs. Behind her, the eighth-grade girls started practicing a cheer routine Teffy knew from Bulldogs games.

Thirty girls. What had she gotten herself into? Teffy tried to keep her fear to herself even though her stomach was doing somersaults. She'd promised herself she'd try new things in middle school, and if all the Taylors made the team together, cheerleading would be a lot of fun.

TS put her hands on her hips and looked around. "Not to worry, girls. I'm going to make sure we all make the squad. We just need to work hard and stick together."

"Yes, Coach TS!" Tay Tay said nice and loud, not caring if she drew stares. "So how does this all work?"

"So, fifth- and sixth-grade girls make up one squad, and seventh- and eighth-grade girls make up the other," Taylor explained as she stretched one of her hamstrings. "The eighth graders help lead the tryouts and scout potential cheerleaders." She used two fingers to point at each of them. "Someone is always watching, so be alert."

Great, Teffy thought. She had to be "on" all the time—something she wasn't. Ever.

"I have to remember that," Taylor added, twirling a

strand of her dark hair around one of her fingers. "My sister says I come across sort of gruff sometimes so I have to watch myself."

"You?" TS teased. "Never."

Taylor rolled her eyes. "I know. I'm working on it, especially since cheerleaders are supposed to be friendly and stuff."

"You were friendly to us," Tay Tay said gently. "We'll help you."

"We'll help each other," TS seconded.

"Good," Teffy said, staring to sweat. "Because I'm getting really nervous."

"Don't be. This is just a meeting." TS motioned for them to follow her. "Come on. Let's get good seats so we can hear everything."

The Taylors took their seats on the bleachers. They talked quietly until a petite young woman with brown hair wearing athleisure came bounding down the bleacher steps and stood in the front of the crowd. Teffy knew from Charlie that this was Ms. Cherie, a seventh- and eighth-grade math teacher who coached the cheer squads.

"Good afternoon, Harrison!" Ms. Cherie shouted with her

hands on her hips, looking like she was about to launch into a routine.

There was a raucous cheer. Teffy felt her stomach roll again.

"It's amazing to see so many of you are interested in cheer-leading for Harrison Middle School this year, so let me explain how this all works. We will have two squads: seventh/eighth grade and fifth/sixth-grade one," Ms. Cherie told the group, just as Taylor had said. "Cheer is not only a great way to make new friends at Harrison, but also a great way to move your body, reduce stress, and boost confidence. What other after-school activity gives you the chance to stand in front of packed bleachers every Saturday afternoon?"

"I usually have soccer games Friday night, so this would work!" whispered TS excitedly.

Hannah spun around in front of them. "Shh!" she said as loudly as possible.

"Thank you, Aimee!" Taylor smiled with her teeth.

"You know my name is Hannah." She blinked in confusion, which made all the Taylors giggle.

Suddenly, there were whoops and hollers and a group of seventh- and eighth-grade girls stepped out to the center of the gym in formation. They wore navy-and-white cheer uniforms: tank tops with a small bulldog insignia on the top right and short navy skirts with glitter trim on the bottom. Every girl was wearing crisp white sneakers that had navy glitter laces on them, and girls with long hair had their tresses tied back with big navy-and-white glitter bows. The girls were all ethnicities, shapes, and sizes, but they looked confident, happy, and brave—like Teffy wanted to be.

Teffy decided then and there she'd never wanted to be a cheerleader more in her life.

"Please welcome some of the leaders of our seventh-and-eighth-grade squad," Ms. Cherie said by way of introduction. All the girls cheered loudly. "Paola and Taryn will be leading you through a routine this afternoon that you will be expected to perform during tryouts next week." There was nervous laughter around the gym. "Don't worry. You're not expected to know this by the end of today. We will be holding three days of tryouts and we will be making cuts," Ms. Cherie informed them, "so learn this routine well, and get your game faces on. We want energy. Personality! Enthusiasm! And we are looking not only for girls with technique but who are also team players. The word *cheerleader* says it all—we want you to be able to cheer and also lead."

Personality? Technique? Enthusiasm? Teffy wasn't sure what part of this tryout process was going to be hardest. She hoped dance class coupled with practicing the moves to some of the routines from the Eras Tour counted. She started to pick at her nails nervously.

"We are going to move fast and have a lot of fun," Ms. Cherie added. "Are you ready?"

Teffy felt her heart start thumping in her chest as she cheered along with the other Taylors. The other three Taylors didn't look nervous at all.

"Now, before we stand and divide you into groups to work with our older cheerleaders to learn the first routine, I do have to tell you that competition will be fierce," Ms. Cherie added. "While eighty-five of you are on the sign-up sheet I have in front of me, we will only be able to take twenty-four girls on each squad." The room grew quiet.

Twenty-four girls from fifth and sixth grade. Twenty-four from seventh and eighth.

That was six fewer girls than Taylor thought the squad would take. It meant a little more than half the girls seated in the gym right now would actually make it.

Teffy clutched her stomach self-consciously and tried not to think about the odds.

"So give it your all during tryouts and let's get out there and have fun!" Ms. Cherie said, and all the cheerleaders started to applaud and do kicks and lots of cheerlead-y stuff.

"Let's have everyone rise and we will divide you into six groups," said one of the cheerleaders. "First two rows follow me."

"That's us," TS said, jumping up. Tay Tay and Taylor were already running ahead. "Let's get a good spot so we can see what we're doing."

Teffy's heart dropped. Hannah and Greta were also in their group. *Great.*

TS must have seen Teffy's expression because she grabbed her hand. "Don't worry. I've got your back. We can do this together, okay?"

Teffy nodded. "Okay." She didn't know TS well yet, but she could already tell she would be a good friend. She was always thinking of others and she was a great coach. She squeezed TS's hand back and felt a little more at ease. They jogged over to Taylor and Tay Tay.

"My sister said the first routine you learn is the simplest so if you can slay that, you get the basics down and go from there," Taylor told them. "I am pretty sure I know the first routine already so I can teach it to all of you later."

Teffy got in line with the three other Taylors. Hannah and Greta were in the row in front of them. Teffy tried to ignore them.

"Hi, everyone! I'm Paola," said the cheerleader in front of their group. She had a warm smile, long dark hair she wore in a ponytail, and her olive skin sparkled with silver body glitter. "First, we'll do the routine a few times without music, then I'll play a recording of the band we usually perform with." There was nervous energy from the group. "We'll take it slow. Ready?" She placed her feet together, and her hands on her hips. "Right step, two, three, four, now turn, two, three, four!"

For the next fifteen minutes, the Taylors watched and copied every move Paola made. When Paola sidestepped and clapped, they sidestepped and clapped. When Paola jumped, they jumped. The entire time Paola was teaching, she would call out steps, timed in sets of eight. Teffy got some of the steps, but others were tricky.

"One, two, three, four, five, six, seven, eight," Paola said, showing the timed moves over and over again.

"Oops!" Teffy said, turning on four instead of on five and crashing into the girl in front of her. "Sorry!"

"It's okay," said the girl, but Hannah wasn't as forgiving.

"Watch it," she said with a huff. "I don't need you messing me up."

Teffy felt her face burn. Of course, Hannah picked up the whole routine the first time Paola ran it.

"Ignore her." Taylor glared at Hannah now. "We're all just learning."

Paola looked over. When she noticed Taylor's expression, she frowned.

"Smile," Teffy whispered, nudging her, and Taylor seemed to realize what was happening. She grinned big and wide. Paola nodded approvingly. "But thanks," Teffy added. She could feel her heart pumping, sweat beading on her brow, and it was hard to talk without taking breaths, but she just kept going.

"No problem," said Taylor, who looked a bit anxious now too.

Even Tay Tay, who had the loud cheer part down, was struggling with some of the dance moves. As was TS, who claimed she'd never danced a day in her life. By the time Paola showed them an elaborate "ball change, pivot, and split" move, all the Taylors were exhausted.

"Now, let's speed it up and put it to the music," Paola told the group. "And I want to hear you cheer nice and loud."

Uh-oh, Teffy thought.

With music, it was a lot harder. Remembering the cheer on top of the steps was complicated too. Counting out the steps in her head didn't work as well when she was rushing through them. But she wasn't alone. Most of the other girls in their group got turned around, a few banging into one another. One girl fell. Another accidentally hit someone in the face.

"It's okay," Paola told them. "No one gets it on the first try."

By the tenth try, Teffy realized something important: Cheerleading was way harder than she thought it would be.

"How are you all feeling?" Ms. Cherie asked with just as much enthusiasm now as she had before practice started an hour ago.

The cheer that followed was definitely a bit weaker.

"By the time you get home tonight, we'll have emailed each of you a link to the routine's music so that you can practice at home, and I do recommend you practice," Ms. Cherie said, looking around the room. "If you had fun today, and you want on this squad, this is the way to make it happen—know that routine backward and forward so there is no doubt you belong on one of the Harrison cheer squads. You're all dismissed!"

Girls started filing out and Teffy couldn't help but hear snippets of their conversation. There were way too many people saying "that was easy" for her liking. Nothing about learning that routine was easy. Or smiling the whole time or shouting the chant nice and loud while maintaining high kicks. All to music! Teffy took a deep breath.

What would Taylor do?

And she didn't mean herself.

She meant *the* Taylor.

Teffy had to imagine Taylor practiced her routines for countless hours before she nailed them. She had read somewhere that Taylor practiced singing all her songs on the treadmill so she could have the stamina to dance through a three-plus-hour show. This routine was less than five minutes long. Teffy could do this.

"This is way harder than I thought it would be. I don't know if I can do this," Tay Tay said, turning to the others. "I've got the stamina, and I can do the kicks and splits, but the actual routine trips me up."

"Yeah, but you're the loudest cheerer here," TS pointed out. "That's a good thing. I can do the steps but not well, and I can't remember the words to the chants. Are we yelling 'Go, Bulldogs' or 'Goat Bulldogs'?"

"Why would we yell 'Goat Bulldogs'?" Teffy said with a laugh.

TS's blue eyes sparkled. "It's more fun."

"At least they don't think you're grumpy," Taylor interjected. "I can help you with the routine and the words, but I need help with the actual 'cheer' part of cheerleading. I think my crankiness is going to be my downfall." She glanced at Teffy. "Unlike Teffy. Your smile is better than anyone's here. You haven't let it fall. Not even once. You've got cheerleader mode down."

Teffy grinned shyly. "Thanks, but a smile isn't going to get me on the team." She looked at the others. "My kicks are good, but I keep messing up the routine."

"I've made a decision: We will have a group practice," TS announced. "Or several group practices. Or an all-day practice. We won't stop till we are perfect and—"

"We need a sleepover!" Tay Tay burst out, practically shouting and dancing around at the thought. "We can have it at my house. My dad has been begging to meet my friends." She bit her lip. "We are friends now, aren't we?"

"Yes, we're friends!" said TS, hugging her. "Great idea!"

Friends. As in more than one. She wasn't just surviving middle school, she was killing it. Okay, slight exaggeration, but it was going well, wasn't it? *Next step is to make the team,* Teffy thought. *Getting on the squad is going to be hard, but maybe with the Taylors' help, I can make it happen.*

"I can come Saturday since I don't have practice, but don't you have to ask first?" TS asked, snapping the rubber bracelet around her wrist that said GOALS.

Tay Tay pulled out her phone and texted fast. Seconds later, she was grinning. "My dad said yes." She looked at the others. "What do you say? I have a pool and we can sleep in the den and watch the Eras Tour movie and sing Taylor's songs and—"

"We need to practice a lot," TS reminded her.

"Yes, we will practice. Tons!" Tay Tay said, bouncing on her toes. "So you'll all come?"

"Definitely," said TS.

"Yes," said Taylor.

Everyone looked at Teffy.

She'd had sleepovers with her cousins, but never one with friends before. Would her mom and dad say yes? She'd beg. She'd let her mom call Tay Tay's dad to introduce herself and then drop her off. She could convince her. Her first sleepover with friends. It sounded like so much fun. Teffy grinned. "I'm in too!"

EIGHT

Call It What You Want

At two p.m. on Saturday, Teffy was in the car with her mom on the way to Tay Tay's house with her sleeping bag, a pillow, and her overnight bag that had the words A LOT GOING ON AT THE MOMENT stamped on the side of it. She had also brought a tray full of cupcakes that she'd made herself. They were frosted in pink and blue pastels, and on each cupcake she'd used an edible frosting pen to write the letter *T*.

Clearly, she was all about a theme.

The cupcakes looked great, but she was still nervous. A sleepover meant a lot of time together, and truthfully, she still barely knew the other Taylors.

A sleepover will change all that, she told herself.

"I still can't believe there are three other Taylors in your home-room," her mom said as she followed the car navigation to Tay Tay's house. "And that they got you to try out for cheerleading."

"I'm as surprised as you are." Teffy grinned. "But I've decided middle school is the time to try new things."

Her mom gaped. "Who are you and what have you done with my Teffy?" They both laughed. "Good for you, sweetie! I'm proud of you."

"Thanks," Teffy said, even if her stomach was a jumble of nerves about both tryouts and tonight's sleepover.

"Do you know if the other Taylors are going to the concert?" her mom asked, her voice sounding slightly strained.

Teffy knew her mom searched the resale sites for tickets daily. She even overheard her mom telling Liam's mom how bad she felt that the prices were too high to even consider. Teffy didn't want to tell her mom about the plan she and Tay Tay came up with to save up for tickets either. It might not happen, and she didn't want her mom to feel bad either way. "They don't have tickets yet either," she said. "But this girl Hannah at my old lunch table went to Amsterdam to see her, and Taylor Perez says Hannah spent five thousand dollars a ticket for floor seats at the Indianapolis show."

"Her parents paid five thousand a ticket?" her mom screeched, hitting the brakes a little hard at the stop sign. "That is just ridiculous. You understand that, Teffy, don't you? Spending that much money for a ticket to a concert you can stream and watch at home is just . . . wow."

Five thousand dollars for a concert ticket did sound bonkers, but watching Taylor at home was not the same thing. Teffy didn't want to hurt her mom's feelings though. "I know, Mom."

"I'm just making sure. I'm going to keep looking, honey. And if we can't get tickets, I will still take you to the arena to tailgate. Mrs. Yoon said her niece did it in Philadelphia and they could hear the whole concert. They had a lot of fun. Have you seen the videos of the fans on the hill in Munich?"

She had. "Those were amazing." Tay Tay had shown her on her phone. And no, listening outside the stadium still wasn't the same thing, but she'd at least be breathing the same air. "Tay-Gating will be fun," she said, trying to sound enthusiastic.

Her mom smirked. "*Tay*-Gating?"

"That's what people call it," Teffy said knowingly, and thought of something. "Do you think the other Taylors can join us? If they don't get tickets either?"

"That's a great idea," her mom said.

The navigation announced they'd reached Tay Tay's block. A few seconds later, they pulled up in front of a huge new house.

Behind it, Teffy saw the edges of Sweet Greens Christmas Tree Farm, giant fir trees looking like a forest.

"You can mention it to the girls at the sleepover," her mom said as they got out of the car. "And listen, if for any reason you're not having fun, or you want to come home, just text me."

"I'm sure I'll be fine," Teffy told her mom as she balanced her bag and cupcakes.

"I know, but if not, don't worry. We will get you any time." Her mom came around the car, taking her pillow and bag from her to walk up the flower-lined path. "You know what? We can have a code, like a letter you text, so no one knows what you're talking about."

"And I'll text you from my iPad," Teffy said as a little dig, which wasn't like her, but being the girl without a cell phone was something she still felt weird about.

But her mom missed the point. "We will ask Mr. Johnson for his Wi-Fi so you'll have no issues." The door opened before Teffy could respond and Mr. Johnson and Tay Tay smiled, the perfect welcoming committee. Mr. Johnson was tall, like Tay Tay, and was dressed in shorts and a graphic tee, which was funny to see on a dad.

"Hi! You must be Teffy, am I right?" he said by way of greeting. "I've heard so much about you." He shook her mom's hand. "I'm Bryan. Thanks for letting Teffy stay with us tonight."

"Thank you for having her," her mom said. "Teffy told me you recently moved from Florida?"

"Flori-da!" Teffy and Tay Tay sang loudly on cue. Everyone laughed.

As the two parents continued talking, Tay Tay motioned for Teffy to follow her into the kitchen. Teffy could see from the kitchen all the way through to the den, where big French doors overlooked a pool, and beyond the fence, the famed Christmas tree farm. Tay Tay's house smelled like fresh paint—and all the furniture looked like it was out of a catalog. Teffy thought of her own house, which was worn down and lived-in. She felt a little funny, but she reminded herself, friends don't judge. Tay Tay would probably love her house just as much.

"These cupcakes look ah-mazing!" Tay Tay said, taking the tray and placing it next to a plate of cookies and brownies. "We'll leave it all in here so it doesn't melt. The other Taylors are already outside."

Teffy dropped her stuff with the other girls' packs in the

den, and followed Tay Tay outside. She couldn't wait to swim. The August heat was brutal. The backyard was equally nice—a massive pool with a pool house and an inflatable swan. Music was playing softly through the speakers (guess who?) and Taylor and TS were both seated under an umbrella on a wicker couch. When they saw Teffy, both jumped up.

TS clapped her hands. "TEFFFFFFFF-EEEEE! You're here! Guess what? I scored the winning goal at my soccer scrimmage. We won! And now we will win cheerleading! Let practice begin!" She tried reciting the cheer they'd learned at the meeting and did a goofy dance to go along with it. Black marks were still smudged beneath her eyes from her soccer game earlier.

"Hey! You're getting better," Taylor marveled, sitting down at the edge of the pool and kicking her feet in the water. She pulled her dark hair into a knot and stuck it on top of her head with a hair tie. "And look at me!" She smiled big and pointed to her super-white teeth.

"Maybe we should swim then practice. It is too hot." Tay Tay pulled off her pink tee and jumped right into the pool. "Cannonball!" She made a huge splash.

"Hey!" Taylor said, laughing. "You got me wet!"

"Get in!" Tay Tay said, and suddenly TS was jumping in the pool followed by Taylor. Teffy quickly pulled off her shorts and tee, revealing her green bathing suit, and jumped in after them.

"This is so nice," TS said, grabbing the swan float and hopping on. Taylor climbed on behind her and the two balanced to keep from falling off. "I could live in this pool."

"We have to get out to practice eventually," Taylor said, but she looked equally happy.

"And plot the Taylors' world domination," TS said decisively.

Tay Tay cheered super loud. "YES! The Taylors for the win!"

"You definitely have the lungs to be a cheerleader," Taylor joked, holding her ears.

"Do you think we should tell Mr. Ball our nicknames?" Teffy asked the group.

"Yes," Tay Tay agreed, hitting an inflatable ball to Teffy, who volleyed it back. "Think of how much easier it will be writing our nicknames instead of first name/last initial all the time."

TS spiked the ball back in Teffy's direction. She hit it to Taylor. "All we need now is a Taylors catchphrase."

"Catchphrase?" Teffy asked, confused.

"You know, for when we need team spirit," TS explained. "All the teams I'm on have them. Something we can do together like a secret handshake or we all throw our hands in a circle and say something powerful to psych us up."

All the girls thought for a moment. Teffy heard music from a speaker in the backyard and realized "Delicate" was playing. That gave her an idea. "You know how everyone at the concerts chants during 'Delicate,' like 'One, two, three . . . Let's go'? What if we did 'One, two, three . . . Let's go, Taylors'?"

"YES!" Tay Tay said, jumping up and down in the water and creating waves. "Let's try it. Hands in!" She put her hand out and Teffy put her hand on top of Tay Tay's. TS and Taylor leaned over too far to try to do the same and fell off the swan with a big splash. Everyone laughed as they swam over and each put their hand on top of Teffy's. All four girls looked at one another.

"Ready?" TS said.

All the girls responded.

"One, two, three, let's go, Taylors!" they shouted, and threw their hands in the air.

Teffy smiled so hard her mouth hurt. This sleepover was so much fun already and it was just getting started.

NINE
Everything Has Changed

With their catchphrase secured and a cool-off accomplished, Taylor decided to FaceTime her sister Maddie to ask for the inside scoop on tryouts.

"Look, it's not necessarily who is the best at every cheer, stunt, and routine," explained Maddie, a girl with long dark hair, light brown skin, and big brown eyes. She was Taylor's mirror image, just older (and she smiled way more). "Ms. Cherie wants to see how you can be leaders. How creative you are. How well you can follow directions and work together. So yeah, practice your splits, and make sure you have the cheer down, but then try to make the routine your own."

Someone mumbled something in the background.

"Oh, right," said Maddie to whoever she was talking to off-screen. "Make it your own but don't go too off-script. Just give the routine your own style. Good luck!"

"Thanks, Mads," said Taylor, before ending the video call. Then she looked at the others and frowned. "So be less me . . . but also more me?"

TS laughed. "She means be a team player. Ms. Cherie said that at the meeting. She doesn't want one person trying to be the best, she wants us all to be good."

"Hannah, on the other hand . . ." Tay Tay mumbled.

"Forget Hannah," TS insisted. "The four of us are making this squad, so the best thing we can do now is figure out what each of us are good at." She snapped her fingers. "Why don't we each run the routine alone and the rest of us will critique so we know what we each need help with."

"That's a great idea," Tay Tay said, doing a split in the air as practice.

"Alone?" Teffy felt her stomach somersault. *A critique? This is my worst nightmare.*

"Hey," TS scolded. "Cheerleaders don't whine. Or worry."

Teffy gave her a fake smile.

"Better. Act like you've made it and you will. Ready? I'll go first." TS pulled the music Ms. Cherie sent up on her phone and dove right in. Her steps were perfect.

"Technically all good, but you need some attitude," Tay Tay told her.

"You look like you're counting steps in your head," Taylor told her.

TS laughed. "I am! Okay, I'll work on that. Tay Tay, you're up."

Tay Tay had the opposite problem—she went off-script. A lot.

"Too much improvising," Taylor told her. "I like the added handstand and the second split, but then you did a cartwheel twice and another handstand and it was too much."

"Fair," Tay Tay said, out of breath. "I'll dial it back. Taylor, you're up."

Taylor tried to show enthusiasm when she ran the number, but her expressions made it look like someone was forcing her to perform.

"Ummmm," hedged Tay Tay.

"Your smile is rigid and so are your arms. See?" said TS, unafraid to show Taylor a recording of herself.

Taylor groaned. "I look like a robot."

"A cute robot," TS said sweetly. "I'm sending everyone their video so we each know what to work on when we're not together. Teffy, you're up."

Teffy had been avoiding giving feedback because she was afraid of what her friends would say when it was her turn. And now it was. Her stomach flip-flopped as she stood at the edge of the pool and turned to face the Taylors. *You can do this,* she told herself.

TS started the music and Teffy ran the routine. The whole thing lasted a few minutes, but it felt like an hour. When she was done, she looked at the others.

"Dance-wise, you're perfect," Tay Tay said, "but your voice needs more . . . needs more . . ."

"You sound like a mouse," Taylor said bluntly. They all nudged her. "She does! I can't hear you, Teffy. Cheerleaders need to *cheer*. I'm one to talk, but I'm loud at least."

Teffy covered her face with her hands. "I'm hopeless."

"No, you're not," TS said. "We are going to make this happen. We still have the whole afternoon and tonight and tomorrow morning together. We are whipping the Taylors into shape!"

"Yeah!" Tay Tay cheered. "Let's get to work!"

"Thank you, Tay Tay," TS said, matching her enthusiasm with a high kick. "We've got spirit, how about you? We've got spirit! Yes, we do! You try, Teffy!"

Teffy froze. "Now?"

Taylor came up next to her and whispered in her ear. "Try closing your eyes. Pretend you're home in your room and then repeat the cheer in your head."

That wasn't a bad idea. Teffy thought of the safety of her bedroom and the picture of Taylor on her mirror. *No one is watching*, she told herself. *Pretend you're practicing by yourself and only your Taylor picture is there to see it.* Teffy took a deep breath. "WE'VE GOT SPIRIT!"

"Whoa!" TS and Tay Tay held their ears.

"Don't shout it. Just be loud," said Tay Tay.

"There's a difference?" Teffy asked. They all nodded. She closed her eyes and tried again. "We've got spirit! Yes, we do!" she said with enthusiasm.

"Yes!" TS clapped. "Now if only I could stop counting steps."

"I can help you with that," Teffy said. "Take it one line at a time and practice each step with that line. I like to write it down and then I keep writing it over and over till I know it by heart."

TS thought for a moment. "I'll try it. Tay Tay? Do you have paper?"

"Do I have paper?" Tay Tay did a cartwheel over to the table in the back, coming dangerously close to the edge of the pool. She held up a pad. "Here you go. Now, can someone help me learn the steps?"

"I can help you with those," Taylor offered, "if you watch my expression and make sure it's friendly enough."

"Deal," said Tay Tay.

The Taylors divided and conquered for the next hour; retreating to opposite ends of the yard, Teffy working on projecting, practicing the cheer words and steps with TS while Taylor and Tay Tay helped each other with the routine itself and Taylor's emoting. Teffy had never spent this much time with just TS before. She was funny and quirky (her love of cats, obscure cartoons, and decorating everything she owned with glitter ran deep). TS was also a good listener.

"You can't let Hannah get to you," TS said. "She's like Dark Master Mulder, the villain in my favorite comic." Teffy must have looked confused because TS went on: "You have to read it, but since you haven't, I'll explain: Mulder preys on people's fears." She paused. "And then literally eats their thoughts." She waved her hand in the air, her friendship bracelets banging together. "It's a whole thing. I'll give you a comic to borrow.

But that's Hannah! If she thinks you don't care, she won't either. I'm telling you."

"Okay. I'll try that." Teffy looked across the yard at Tay Tay and Taylor working together. "Thanks for listening. I feel weird bringing this up with everyone."

TS smiled. "Your secret is safe with me."

"Hey! You two! Look at Taylor!" Tay Tay yelled across the pool.

Taylor was running the routine with a huge smile on her face. A smile that was neither creepy nor forced. It was joyful. Teffy and TS started to cheer.

"And I have the routine down with some extra flair, but not too much." Tay Tay mock bowed and they all applauded her.

"Hey, mermaids!" Tay Tay's dad came out the back door carrying a tray of food. "Who's hungry?"

"Me!" they all said, and clamored to the outdoor kitchen that had an island with stools. Mr. Johnson had ordered hamburgers and fries from a local place and gotten a massive veggie platter with hummus and pita chips. When he opened the mini fridge and offered the girls three types of water—sparkling, flavored, or flat—Teffy was in awe. Tay Tay said her dad was in business and worked for a bank, but clearly, he made a lot of money.

"How was rehearsal?" he asked the girls.

"We are all improving," Tay Tay told him. "We can do a run-through for you after dinner if you want." She opened her eyes wide. "Ooh! Or do you think the Tremonts will turn on the lights and let us dance in Sweet Greens? The farm would be so inspiring."

"I'll text them. I'm sure they wouldn't mind." The girls all cheered as he went inside.

"Your dad is the coolest," TS announced to the group.

"I know," agreed Tay Tay. "Even if he couldn't get Taylor concert tickets from work." Her face fell. "His company has a suite at Lucas Oil, but he wasn't senior enough to get any tickets. He knows I want to go so badly, but he thinks it's ridiculous what people are paying for tickets online." She looked at Teffy. "I guess if we really want to see Taylor, we're on our own."

"It's okay," said Teffy, trying not to sound disappointed. "I am manifesting we find a way to get them."

"You know, I was thinking about your plan," Taylor said, sounding suddenly shy. "All of us want to see Taylor, and none of us have enough money on our own. I know you two are trying to get tickets together, but what if all four of us pooled our money? I mean, if you don't mind me and TS getting in on this scheme."

"Are you kidding?" Tay Tay nudged Taylor. "Of course we want you to come."

"All of us seeing Taylor together would be the best day ever," Teffy had to admit. Dare she even dream it could happen?

Taylor's smile was so genuine, Teffy wished she could record it. "Okay, I'm in then!" Taylor said. "I have some birthday money saved up we could use."

"So do I," said TS. She glanced at Teffy. "Imagine how much money we could raise with all four Taylors plotting together!" They all looked at one another, their smiles getting wider and wider.

"This is going to be EPIC!" Tay Tay burst out.

"First, we need a plan," Taylor said, and looked directly at Teffy as if she knew Teffy would have one.

The wheels in Teffy's brain were already turning. "The Taylors Get Taylor Tickets Plan," Teffy said, putting down her hamburger and reaching for the pad and paper to start writing things, "starts now."

TS rubbed her hands together. "I never lose. We are making this happen. I'm thinking we call into every contest on satellite radio and try to win tickets. And research different giveaways— I'm sure someone is giving away Taylor tickets to raise money for a charity."

"Contests and raffles. Good idea," Teffy said, writing the idea down and TS's name next to it.

"I guess becoming backup dancers is out?" Tay Tay said, dancing in her seat.

"Yes, but you still might be on to something," Taylor said, snapping her fingers. "What if there was a way to get Taylor's attention?"

"How?" TS asked.

"Taylor donates to causes all the time—she helped refurbish her high school auditorium. She donated money to New York City Public Schools. She gives to food banks. She does the hat thing all the time at the Eras shows."

"The hat . . ." Teffy said wistfully. "I dream about that moment. Taylor walking down the catwalk right to me where I'm waiting, singing my heart out as she kneels down and places that hat on my head. And then I hand her a friendship bracelet I made."

"I have that dream too," said Tay Tay with a sigh.

"Same," TS and Taylor echoed.

"I'm all for getting her attention, but we are not a cause or a charity she needs to help," TS reminded them. "Taylor does those things because she's a good person. She's been volunteering for things since she was our age. Last year my mom and I signed up for Global Youth Service Day because of her and volunteered at an animal shelter."

Teffy clutched her heart. "Can we all go do that this year?" They nodded.

"Lots of fans want tickets. If we make her a video, what are we saying exactly? What makes us special?"

Taylor smiled. "We are friends named Taylor after Taylor Swift and our name and love of Taylor brought us together. It's not deserving, but it *is* cool."

TS chewed on a celery stick. "That is true."

"Taylor does a lot of giving back, yes, but she also just loves doing things for her fans," Taylor pointed out. "Think of the clues and hints before album drops and all the Easter eggs and bonus tracks in the middle of the night! She loves us as much as we love her. So, as my mom would say, getting tickets is a want, not a need, but I still think if we could find a way to tell Taylor the story of how we became friends—she'd like it."

"It's worth a shot," Tay Tay said, warming up to the idea. "Maybe we could make a video and post it online."

"I'm not allowed social media," TS blurted out, her cheeks turning red.

"Neither am I," Teffy admitted. *I also don't even have a phone.*

"That's okay," Tay Tay said. "I can post it for us. If that's okay."

TS and Teffy looked at each other. Was it okay? Would their parents be mad? Teffy felt funny telling the others she had to ask for permission.

"Ask them," Tay Tay said. "If they say no, we can come up with other ways to get Taylor's attention."

"But we can't just wish and hope Taylor sees our video," TS said. "We should come up with real ways to buy tickets too." She paused. "You know what? We should make a pact—we get tickets together or not at all. If someone finds two tickets, the answer is no. We need four."

"I like that idea," Teffy spoke up, and the others nodded in agreement. Seeing Taylor would be amazing. But seeing Taylor with her friends named Taylor would be unbelievable. "Although, we need five tickets, not four. Someone's parent has to take us."

"They'll have to battle it out to be the chaperone," TS joked. "But I know people who got six tickets, so it's not impossible to find five."

"No, it's not," said Tay Tay giddily. "I can't imagine going with anyone other than you three anyway."

"You're going to make me cry," TS said, pretending to sniffle. "But *same*."

"Win raffles and make a Taylor Swift video," Taylor interrupted. "What else can we do? We need a way to make money."

"What if we make bracelets and sell them?" Teffy asked, showing off her friendship bracelets on her arm. "I know they're cheap, but if we sell enough of them, we could do it."

"I like it," said TS, grinning wickedly. "I say we even compete to see who can make the most in one night."

"You're so competitive!" Taylor laughed. "But it's a good idea. The more we make, the more we sell, and the more money we have."

"Does everyone here make friendship bracelets?" Teffy asked.

The other three girls held up their arms to show off their bracelets.

Taylor laughed. "Okay, I'm the only one who doesn't, but my sister does and she'll give me her kit. We can make them and sell them to everyone we know."

"Yes!" TS agreed. "Good plan."

"This is going to work," said Tay Tay, excited now.

Teffy was too. All hope was not lost. There was a still a chance they'd get tickets. Four people trying to get them was better than one, right? "I've got a good feeling about this."

"We've got sixty-nine days till Taylor comes to Indianapolis," Taylor told them. "Let's make this happen."

THE TAYLORS GET TAYLOR TICKETS PLAN

<u>Our Awesome List of Ways We're Going to Get Tickets to See</u>

<u>Taylor Swift's Eras Tour at Lucas Oil Stadium</u>*

*And who is in charge of each idea

1. Make video for Taylor telling her how we're named after her and how we're all friends and would give anything to go to the concert (Taylor's idea)

2. Find raffles giving away tickets—check all the local sports teams and schools. Check for radio giveaways (TS is in charge of this one)

3. Make friendship bracelets and sell them to cover ticket costs (Teffy's specialty, but everyone can help)

4. Ask every parent, friend, grandparent, store owner, and human in Indianapolis if they know of anyone selling tickets that we can afford* (Tay Tay)

*Code for anything less than $300 a ticket

TEN

Breathe

As luck would have it, cheerleading auditions were postponed when Ms. Cherie caught a stomach bug along with half the eighth grade. The Taylors spent the bonus practice time perfecting their tryout. Teffy was even brave enough to perform her cheer for her parents in the backyard over Labor Day weekend.

"We've got spirit, yes we DO!" Teffy faced her parents, who were sitting in lawn chairs, looking on encouragingly. "I mean . . . We've GOT SPIRIT . . . uh . . ."

Teffy could hear her voice going up and down like someone had grabbed the TV remote and couldn't decide on the volume. *Get it together, Teffy,* she told herself. "WE'VE . . ." *Nope. Too loud.* "GOT!" *Too enthusiastic.* "We've?" *Too low and your voice cracked.*

"Keep going," her dad said while her mom smiled wide, trying to be positive.

And then Teffy caught sight of someone out of the corner of her eye.

Charlie and Alex Yoon were crouched down in the bushes watching her.

This time, Teffy had no trouble getting her lungs to work.

"DAD!" She pointed to the culprits, and they ran off laughing. Teffy felt her face burn, her stomach slosh around like she was at sea. "If they recorded me, I swear . . ."

"Don't worry," her mom said, her voice steely as she stood up fast and watched the boys run into the Yoons' yard. "We've had lengthy conversations with Charlie about how inappropriate it is to record *anyone* without their permission." She paused. "But I'm going to go remind both boys. I'll be right back."

Teffy covered her face with her hands and breathed deeply, trying to still herself. How was she still not getting this? Tryouts began this Tuesday and she didn't feel ready. It didn't help she was still letting Hannah get in her head every chance she got.

All week long, Hannah had been bragging to anyone in class who would listen about how good she was at cheerleading. How her parents had bought her the latest phone "just because."

How she might go to one of Taylor's Miami shows too. "Too bad you're not going to any of her shows, Teffy," Hannah had said when she caught Teffy listening one day during snack. "You must be so jealous."

"Ignore her," TS had said when they went to the bathroom together during class. "I told you—I think she's worse to you because she knows she gets under your skin."

While Tay Tay's energy was so effusive and fun to be around, and Taylor was the most loyal friend in the world, TS was the easiest to confide in. Teffy had even told TS how she spoke to the Taylor Swift photo on her mirror. TS admitted she did the same thing, only with a picture of soccer star Alex Morgan.

And while, yes, it turned out Teffy really was the only Taylor without a cell phone, TS understood how hard it was being one of the few people they knew who wasn't allowed to use social media. ("My mom says I don't need it, and while I don't want to tell her she's right, I kind of don't mind," TS confided.) Taylor and Tay Tay were allowed to have accounts—set to private and monitored by their parents, who they had to be friends with online—but they didn't make fun. They understood. Both said they really only used it to follow Taylor and watch her videos.

"I'm trying," Teffy told TS. "But I'm nervous about tryouts. If Hannah starts whispering about me or laughs when I cheer, I don't think I could handle it."

"What would Taylor do?" TS demanded. "Tell you to fight for yourself. Don't let anyone make you feel small."

"You're right," Teffy said. *Be bold. Be brave.* Was she forgetting her promise to herself this school year already? Look at all she'd accomplished in just a few short weeks. Not only had she made friends, she had a friend group. One with a name for themselves. She was trying out for a sport. This was a new-and-improved Teffy. Was she really going to let Hannah take that away from her? "I'll do better."

"You're getting so much better!" Teffy's dad said, yanking her from her thoughts. He was wearing a castoff from one of their Harrison by Design logo attempts. "This last time you had real cheerleader energy."

"Thanks, Dad," Teffy said. She knew he was being generous. She'd choked even before she saw Charlie and Alex watching. She had to pull it together.

The phone inside their house started to ring. "I'll get that," her dad said, dashing inside the back door. He came back two seconds later with the cordless phone and held it out to her. "It's for you."

Teffy took the phone and walked over to the other side of the yard—away from Charlie and Alex, who were currently being lectured by her mom. "Hello?"

"Teffy? Good! I found you! Hang on." Tay Tay's voice came over the line. "I'm trying to do a group call. You all there?"

"Here!" said Taylor and TS.

"This couldn't wait till tomorrow," Tay Tay said, sounding out of breath. "We just got a huge order for friendship bracelets. Like, huge!"

"How huge?" Teffy asked, holding her breath.

"Two hundred! And there might be more," Tay Tay said, the excitement in her voice growing. "My dad's boss wants them for his daughter's sweet sixteen and my dad mentioned we were looking for ways to make money to buy tickets to the Eras concert, so he said he'd hire us. We have a month to make them and then, get this: He'll pay us two dollars a bracelet."

"We're going to make four hundred dollars?" TS asked. "That's amazing!"

"It's not enough to buy five tickets though," Taylor said glumly.

"It's a start," Teffy spoke up, because it was. A huge one. "If we do this order, then maybe someone else will see the bracelets and hire us too. We should get started on this order right away." She'd been making Taylor concert–themed ones already for them to sell to friends. "Mrs. Yoon bought six from me already for the concert."

"My dad said he'd buy us some beads in the colors his boss wants," Tay Tay added. "We also need to have his daughter's initials—SC—and the number sixteen on each one. My dad said he's happy to fund our all-important cause.'"

Tay Tay's dad was the greatest. Not that Teffy didn't adore her own dad, but he was always aggravated when he found rogue beads in couch cushions or stepped on one in the kitchen.

"We could have another sleepover next weekend and make a ton together too," TS said. "We can see who can make bracelets the fastest!" The girls laughed. "Plus, we'll have so much to celebrate since we're all making the cheerleading squad."

"Yes, we are," Taylor said with fire in her voice. "You should see me smile. I'm the best smiler ever."

They all laughed.

"I finally memorized the whole chant and am not counting steps," TS told them.

"I think I have the routine down and still have some fun moves in it I can show you all," said Tay Tay.

"I am getting there," Teffy said, not wanting to oversell herself. Today's performance for her parents may have been a bust, but slowly she was finding her voice in fifth grade. Both literally and figuratively. (Hmm . . . She wondered if there was a song she could write about that.)

"Great! I'll ask my dad about the sleepover and text you all tonight," said Tay Tay. "I'm sure he'll say yes."

Teffy felt her stomach start to sway again. Sure, she wanted to have another sleepover with her friends. They'd stayed up till almost two a.m. watching the Eras Tour movie and singing songs till Mr. Johnson said they had to go to sleep or they could never sleep over again (though he said it while he was laughing, so Teffy wasn't sure she believed the threat). But the thought of going to the sleepover and being the only one who didn't make cheerleading . . . Unless it was all four of the Taylors, things were going to be awkward. Still, she bit her lower lip and kept herself from saying anything negative. *Be bold. Be brave.* She clutched the phone tighter and fought off her fears. "Sounds like a plan."

ELEVEN

this is me trying

"And five, six, seven, eight!"

Paola and the other eighth-grade cheerleaders ran though the routine with the fifth- and sixth-grade girls again while Ms. Cherie and two Harrison Middle School teachers handled judging. It was day two of cheerleading auditions and Teffy was exhilarated and exhausted.

Exhilarated because she'd survived day one.

Exhausted because dancing for two hours straight was a lot of work.

Standing in line at the end of the day one session, waiting to hear her name be called to come back for day two had made her want to vomit. Because it wasn't just her name she wanted to hear, it was all the Taylors' names. Thankfully, they'd made it through the cuts, but would she make it to day three? The group was getting smaller. Only twenty-four girls would be chosen:

What were the chances four of them would be the Taylors?

"Nice job, girls!" Ms. Cherie said when they were through. "Take a water break while I talk to Paola."

Teffy's stomach rolled as the eighth-grade captain jogged over to the bleachers to talk to Ms. Cherie. They were whispering and glancing back at the rest of the girls.

"Are they cutting people already?" Tay Tay asked, sounding out of breath.

"No. Are they? We've only been here twenty minutes," said Taylor, sounding flustered. And she never sounded flustered.

"They're definitely discussing something," TS said. "I can see that look in their eye."

"They're making cuts," Teffy said worriedly. "What else could it be?" She balled her hands into fists and took several deep breaths, moving in a circle to release her pent-up energy. A shadow crossed her face.

"Nervous?" Hannah stepped into Teffy's personal space. Today she was wearing a football tee that had the number 13 on it. "I guess I would be too if I were you." Greta, who was with Hannah, couldn't help but snicker.

Teffy would find herself replaying the next few moments for

days. Because instead of firing off a witty comeback or turning on her heels and leaving Hannah and Greta, Teffy froze. And said nothing. She just stood there as Hannah smiled wickedly.

"Everything okay?" Taylor said, appearing at Teffy's side like a bodyguard. "Hey, Hannah."

"Hey, Taylor," Hannah said, her voice dripping with sweetness. "Your kicks are really good. You're definitely going to make the team. I think we both are."

"Me too," Greta said, tugging at Hannah's arm. "Right?"

Hannah made eye contact with Teffy again. "You have nothing to worry about. Unlike some people."

"Not sure who you mean, because all four Taylors are going to make the squad." Taylor grabbed Teffy's arm and yanked her away. "Come on, Teffy. Ignore her."

"Thanks," Teffy whispered, but it was too late. Why had she let Hannah get in her head? She couldn't stop herself now. There were so many other girls who were more qualified, including her friends. Hannah's sister cheered, as did TS's and Taylor's. Tay Tay was a gymnast. They all knew what they were doing. Teffy did not. *I'm getting cut today*, she thought miserably.

"All right, everyone," said Paola, jogging over to the group again. "I spoke to Ms. Cherie and we've decided we're going to break everyone up into groups of four." She pointed to Hannah, Greta, and two sixth graders. "We'll start with you four. When you're done, go sit on the bleachers."

"I forgot they did this," Taylor whispered. "My sister said they do it so they can study each girl up close. That's how they decide who gets cut today."

Uh-oh, Teffy thought.

Ms. Cherie did a cheer clap and everyone repeated it. "Let's give the girls trying out our full attention, ladies." She seemed to be looking at the Taylors when she said that.

Double uh-oh, Teffy thought.

They all turned to watch Hannah, Greta, and the sixth graders. The girls looked flawless as far as Teffy was concerned. The next group moved up, and with this set, Teffy noticed one girl out of sync with the others. She saw Ms. Cherie and the other judges conferring quietly. In the third group, there was a girl who forgot the words. This went on and on till finally Taylor and TS were called over together with two other girls.

"Good luck!" Teffy whispered loudly and gave them a thumbs-up.

Taylor and TS went to the middle of the gym, and Tay Tay and Teffy held hands, watching and worrying. They needn't have. Taylor looked and sounded like a cheerleader! Her energy and attitude were perfect. TS remembered the whole cheer and shouted nice and loud with lots of movement.

"Nice!" Ms. Cherie commented to the group. TS and Taylor high-fived.

"I'm going to get some water before they call us," Tay Tay said. "Stall if I'm not back."

"Okay," Teffy said. She watched TS and Taylor stop and talk to Ms. Cherie for a moment. Everyone was smiling. That had to be a good sign.

"I think we're next, right?" said a girl appearing at her side. She was a sixth grader with curly brown hair tied up in a knot on her head and she was wearing a Harrison Middle School T-shirt and a skort. "I'm going to throw up, I'm so nervous. I don't even know why I did this. I have never danced a day before in my life."

Normally a moment like this would send Teffy diving under the bleachers, but the last few weeks had shown her making small talk with someone didn't have to be scary. She didn't know this girl, but she recognized her from yesterday's tryouts. Most of the girl's friends had been cut the first day. "You must be doing something right. You made it to day two."

"I don't know if I'm going to make it to day three," the girl said with a sigh. "I'm Kristina, by the way."

"Teffy," she said, motioning to herself. "I don't know if I'm going to make it either, but I'm going to try."

Kristina smiled. "Me too."

"Let's get our last group in the center of the gym floor," Paola instructed, and Teffy felt her stomach tighten. She looked over at Taylor and TS on the other side of the gym near Hannah and she tried to look confident, but her nerves were getting the better of her again. She couldn't stop thinking about how badly she'd handled that comment from Hannah.

"Smiles on," Tay Tay whispered, jogging over a moment later. "We've got this."

She pushed her shoulders back and placed her hands on her hips to get ready.

Teffy did the same, giving Kristina a thumbs-up before they moved to the center of the room with Tay Tay and a girl Teffy didn't know. She felt like her lunch was coming up as she stared out at the judges and Ms. Cherie. *Keep it together*, she told herself.

You think Taylor Swift is confident all the time? No. Lights, camera, and smile. Even when you wanna die, she reminded herself.

Paola started the music, and Teffy began the cheer, counting out the steps in her head. The whole routine couldn't be more than a minute, but it felt like an hour. She could hear her voice and it sounded good—loud, but not too loud. She was doing it! Teffy was just getting to the halfway mark, when her eye caught Hannah's and she saw the girl whisper something to Greta. Teffy felt her stomach roll, and distracted, she turned too fast into the next move, crashing into Kristina, who hit Tay Tay and the other girl. All four fell like dominos.

"I'm sorry!" Teffy blurted out, her face warming. She couldn't believe what she'd done. Her chances of making the team were shot and now she'd ruined the other girls' too.

Tay Tay, however, never lost her stride. She jumped right back up and started doing the steps again, as did the other girl, not missing a beat, but Kristina crumbled. She just sat there and placed her hands on her knees. Teffy saw a tear fall down the girl's cheek. Teffy knew she should start the cheer again like the others, but she couldn't leave Kristina down there, not when this was her fault. She leaned down and offered the girl her hand.

"Come on. Let's finish this together," Teffy whispered.

Kristina looked at her hand. "It's too late."

"It's never too late," Teffy decided, and wiggled her fingers at Kristina. Kristina took her hand just as the music stopped and Tay Tay and the other girl finished the routine.

The gym was quiet and everyone was staring. Taylor and TS were watching worriedly. The scene felt like it could be straight out of one of Teffy's nightmares. It would be easy to burst into tears or run out of the gym with everyone staring, but Teffy remembered her mantra: *Smile, even when you wanna die.* "Paola? Could you run it again?" Teffy asked nicely. "Kristina and I want to finish what we started."

Paola glanced at Ms. Cherie. She nodded.

"Go, Teffy and Kristina!" TS cheered, and other girls started to chime in. Their cheering helped Teffy's nerves.

When the music started again, Teffy looked at Kristina encouragingly and they ran the routine again. Teffy wasn't sure it was her best run—her voice was certainly a bit wobbly, but her moves were on point and she smiled the whole time, if not for herself, but for Kristina.

When they finished, many of the cheerleaders cheered.

Ms. Cherie applauded and started whispering with the other judges. Finally, she spoke. "That's it for today, girls. Tomorrow, the names of the girls who have made the two squads will be posted on the gym doors."

Teffy paled. Wait. But Ms. Cherie had said there would be three days of tryouts. Maybe they had changed it after having to postpone? How was she supposed to make things right? Her chest started to tighten.

"Good job today, everyone," Ms. Cherie added. "You're dismissed."

Girls started filing out. Kristina turned to Teffy.

"Thanks for helping me," she said.

"And for knocking you over? Yes, I was a big help," Teffy joked, but she felt terrible.

Kristina's brown eyes were serious. "I mean it. You stuck by me." She glanced in Hannah's direction. "Not everyone would do that. Especially when I have no shot at making the team." Teffy tried to interject, but Kristina waved her off. "It's okay. I can walk on for fall track." She smiled. "And either way, tryouts were fun. I'm glad I met you." She hugged Teffy. "Good luck tomorrow."

"Thanks." Teffy hugged her back. She felt like someone was watching them. When she turned, she saw Ms. Cherie looking from across the room. The cheer coach smiled sympathetically, then turned back to the other judges. Teffy deflated. That was a pity smile. She was not making the squad.

The Taylors walked over. "You okay?" asked TS.

"Not really," Teffy said.

Taylor nudged her. "Stop worrying. You'll be fine."

"Yeah, it was no biggie!" Tay Tay said, cartwheeling out the door.

Teffy sighed. How could two friends be so polar opposite? Tay Tay was a ray of sunshine, and Taylor had stormy days, but neither girl sometimes understood how much Teffy internalized things. Maybe messing up today wasn't a big deal to them, but it was to her.

TS side-hugged her. "Don't worry. It wasn't that bad."

"Liar." Teffy attempted a smile. "I knocked everyone down and asked to run the routine again. There is no way I make the squad."

"Not true," said TS. "You were great with Kristina. That's teamwork. I bet Ms. Cherie saw that and thought if anyone would make a good cheerleader, it's you."

"I don't think it's enough." Teffy spun a friendship bracelet on her wrist.

TS slipped her arm through Teffy's. "You know what might make you feel better right now?"

"What?" Teffy asked as they headed out the gym doors.

"Catching the ice-cream truck before it leaves school grounds. It's on me."

Teffy smiled. The great thing about being one of the Taylors was that there was always someone who got you. And today that someone was TS.

TWELVE

Blank Space

The second the final bell rang after school the following day, there was a mass exodus out of Mr. Ball's class. Girls raced down the hall to the gym doors to read the squad lists—a white list for fifth and sixth grade and a blue list for seventh and eighth graders so there was no confusion.

"Come on!" Tay Tay shouted.

Teffy didn't want to see the list. After stressing all night, Teffy was more convinced than ever she would be the only Taylor not on the squad. The moment she saw that list, reality would set in.

Down the hall, the crowd was growing, girls screaming and throwing their arms around one another, high-fiving as they found their names on the list. Teffy placed a hand over her heart, feeling her chest thumping hard. *Breathe*, she reminded herself. *Just breathe.*

Teffy tried to look confident. *Feel* confident even though she was anything but. Her notebook was burning a hole in her backpack, chock-full of new cheers she had planned to share with Ms. Cherie if she made the squad. After yesterday, those dreams were over.

"Move! Move! Move!" TS shouted to people shuffling down the hallway to their lockers. She weaved in and out of crowds, racing past the other Taylors and reaching the list before them.

"The list isn't going anywhere!" Taylor called after her, then looked at Tay Tay and Teffy. "We can walk slow. I'm sure we all made it."

"*You* did," Teffy said with a sigh.

Tay Tay squeezed her hand. "We'll all look at the list together. Ready?"

Teffy nodded, feeling her stomach roll again. They got to the end of the hall and Teffy watched TS shimmy her way through the other girls, making her way to the doors, her red hair popping up directly in front of the list. She ran her finger down the list of names and started screaming.

Teffy knew what that meant. TS had made it!

"Congrats, TS!" Tay Tay shouted. "What about the rest of us?"

TS grinned. "Come see for yourselves," she shouted over the mayhem.

Taylor rushed over to the list, pushing her way to the front. "YES!" they heard her shout as she pumped her fist in the air.

Teffy's heart was beating faster now. She looked at Tay Tay. "It's okay, you can go look."

"Come with me," Tay Tay said, swinging Teffy's arm.

Teffy shook her head. "I'm going to wait till the crowd dies down."

She didn't want Hannah seeing her look at the list and not find her name.

Tay Tay ran now too, and Taylor and TS made a hole in the crowd so she could get in. Tay Tay started screaming and then busted out some dance moves, making many of the girls laugh. The girls who made the squad started to make their way into the gym while the ones who didn't quietly walked away. Teffy's heart thudded harder and she fought back the urge to cry. She didn't see Kristina anywhere. Maybe Kristina already knew.

"Well?" Tay Tay yelled. "You going to look or not?"

All her friends were grinning. Would they be grinning if she hadn't made the squad? She couldn't have . . . could she? With her palms sweating, her head screaming, and her friends watching, Teffy stepped up to the list. It was easier now that the crowd had thinned out. Her friends stepped aside so Teffy could look.

Teffy ran her finger down the list of names. She didn't see Kristina's, but since she was a "B" name, she didn't have to go far. And there, surprisingly, was her name: Taylor Bennett.

"WHAT?" Teffy shouted, her eyes filling with tears for a different reason now. She looked at the others. "I made the squad!"

"We know!" Tay Tay screamed, and then all the other Taylors, Teffy included, started screaming too. The four grabbed hold of one another, Teffy unsure if she wanted to laugh or cry or both as they hopped up and down in a circle.

"We did it!" TS said again, her face flushed, her smile lighting up her whole face. "The Taylors are Bulldogs cheerleaders!"

The Taylors. All four of them. Teffy couldn't believe it. The girls screamed some more.

"Girls! Girls!" Ms. Cherie appeared behind them, looking amused. "Save the screaming for the football games and get inside. We're going to go over the cheer schedule."

"Sorry," they all mumbled, still giggling as they ran into the gym.

Teffy hung back a second. "Ms. Cherie? Can I ask you something first?"

"Of course." Ms. Cherie was clutching a clear pink clipboard brimming with papers. "What is it?"

"I . . . thought I wasn't going to make the team after what happened yesterday," Teffy admitted. Was she foolish admitting this now?

Ms. Cherie smiled. "That is exactly why you *did* make the team—you fell and got back up again. Not only that, you didn't leave another cheerleader behind. You helped Kristina when she needed it most. We can work on technique, but I want all my cheerleaders to be team players and that's you."

Teffy had goose bumps. "Thank you. I'm going to work hard in there."

"I know you will," said Ms. Cherie. "Let's get in the gym and meet the rest of the squad, shall we?"

Teffy nodded. She was so excited, she felt like she could barely sit still. The meeting didn't last long, thankfully. They learned they'd get their uniforms by week's end and the first game would be this Friday, which worked well for TS, who had a soccer game on Saturday. There were practices after school every day except game days, and the cheer season ran through football and basket-ball seasons, so the girls would be cheering most of the year. Teffy clutched her notebook, which she now knew she'd get up the guts to share with Ms. Cherie at some point. When the meeting was over, Teffy ran into Hannah.

"Congratulations," Teffy said, trying to be friendly.

"Thanks," Hannah said stiffly as she stood with Greta. "I didn't think I'd see you here."

"Guess you were wrong," sang Tay Tay from behind her.

Hannah gave her a look and walked away.

"I don't know why she starts with you," Taylor said with a sigh. "She leaves me alone."

"Because your sisters are friends," said TS, grabbing her bag from the bleachers.

"I guess," said Taylor. "Hannah keeps asking for us all to hang out."

"Do you want to?" Teffy asked, feeling a twinge jealous that Hannah was trying to get in on the Taylors' time together.

Taylor shrugged. "She's not bad. Sometimes." The other Taylors groaned.

"Subject change!" Tay Tay announced, holding up her arm,

which had a dozen bracelets on it. "How many bracelets have you all finished?"

"I did twenty," TS blurted out.

"Whoa," the other Taylors said.

TS grinned wide. "My goal was fifteen and I just had to beat it."

"Of course you did," Teffy laughed. "I stress-beaded and did eight." They all laughed.

"Five?" Tay Tay admitted.

"I only did four," admitted Taylor.

"I win!" TS cheered, doing a few moves. "Let me show you what I made." She pulled a clear bag full of bracelets out of her backpack and showed the girls. They all oohed. The pastel and gold beads looked beautiful together.

"These came out so nice," marveled Teffy. "Now I want one even though we're not going to this party."

"Me too. Ooh! Idea alert," said Tay Tay, bouncing on her toes. "We should make our own. And the lettering can say 'The Taylors.'"

"I love that idea," Teffy agreed, thinking of all four girls with matching bracelets. "Maybe we do a color bead for each of our favorite color."

They were so busy looking at the bracelets, no one noticed Ms. Cherie walk over.

"What are you girls looking at—oh!" She smiled and plucked a bracelet from Teffy's hands. "These are great! Who are they for?"

"My dad hired us to make them for his boss's daughter's sweet sixteen," Tay Tay explained. "We have to make two hundred of them in the next few weeks."

"Two hundred?" Ms. Cherie looked incredulous. "That's a lot."

"Not really," TS bragged. "We're really good at bracelet-making."

"Plus, we're getting paid," Taylor added. "Two dollars a bracelet."

"Nice," Ms. Cherie marveled. "And then you'll split the money?"

"We're saving up to get Taylor Swift tickets together," Teffy told her.

"I'm not sure we can sell enough to buy tickets," Taylor added.

"But we're going to try," said TS with determination.

"Ambitious. I like the motivation." Ms. Cherie sounded impressed. "Taylor Swift tickets do not come cheap."

"Nope, so we have to make a lot," said Teffy.

Ms. Cherie laughed. "I like the confidence, girls." She handed the bracelet back to Teffy. "I have an idea: What if you sold Harrison bracelets and cheer friendship bracelets at games? Might be a great way to make more money."

"We'd love that," said Tay Tay, looking at the other girls in excitement. She squealed when Ms. Cherie walked away. "Think we'll make enough at games to get tickets?"

"Yes," Teffy said decisively. The happiness Tay Tay was feeling was contagious. "If I can make the squad, I think we're capable of anything. We're the Taylors!"

"Yes we are!" Tay Tay cheered and put her hand out.

The others knew exactly what to do.

"One, two, three . . . Let's go, Taylors!" the four girls repeated, throwing their hands in the air.

THIRTEEN

Style

"We are the Bulldogs and we can't be beat, because we've got the power to knock you off your feet!" The Taylors finished the cheer of the game just as the game clock clicked down to zero. Harrison had won their home opener 26–20. Teffy couldn't stop smiling as the football players ran off the field. Waving her pom-pom high in the air, she jumped up and down and did a few kicks while Tay Tay did a perfect cartwheel. Seeing Liam, Teffy waved and he waved back.

Somewhere in the crowd, she knew the Yoons and her parents were watching and would be in the bleachers for hours since Charlie and Alex's eighth-grade team played next. Teffy almost wished she was cheering that game too. Slowly, but surely, she was finding her voice. Who knew getting to shout cheers for two hours would help her confidence? Or that a cheerleading uniform could be so comfy? Her mom had pressed her navy-and-white cheerleading outfit, and all four girls had gotten matching navy bows. Teffy felt so good, she hated the idea of taking the uniform off. The Taylors polished up real nice.

Ms. Cherie gathered round for a quick talk before leaving the bleacher area. "Great job, girls! You look like pros already and tonight was just the start. Now go enjoy the rest of your weekend."

The squad walked over to the bleachers to grab their things, but Ms. Cherie held Teffy back.

"Nice job out there, Teffy," Ms. Cherie said.

"Thank you," Teffy said shyly, her face still flush from cheering and maybe a bit of nerves. She wanted to prove to their coach that choosing her to make the squad wasn't a mistake. Maybe she had.

"I read a few of the cheers you sent me and they're great," Ms. Cherie added. "The one with all the bulldog references? Very clever."

"You really liked it?" Teffy was still getting used to showing anyone her writing. It made her happy Ms. Cherie liked it.

"I was thinking we could test it out this week at practice. Who knows? Maybe we will be ready to use it at the game next weekend," Ms. Cherie added.

"Really? Yes, please!" Teffy threw her arms around her coach, who laughed.

"Keep those cheers coming," Ms. Cherie told her.

"I will! Thank you! Again!" Teffy ran over to the other Taylors, who were watching and waiting. "Ms. Cherie wants to use my Bulldog cheer!"

"Yay!" The girls high-fived her.

"I knew she'd like that one," said TS, who still had black lines painted under her eyes from an early morning soccer practice, which she'd gone to before the Harrison football game. Teffy thought back-to-back sports was a lot, but TS seemed to thrive off it.

"Girls, let's get a picture," said Mrs. Perez, Taylor's mom. The whole family was wearing Bulldogs T-shirts. Taylor's brothers even had the word TAYLOR written in Sharpie on their cheeks. They were so excited for her. Taylor pretended to hate the attention, but Teffy knew her friend was secretly loving it.

"*Mom*, no," Taylor groaned, but she was smiling.

"The quicker you take a picture, the faster you'll get out of here," Teffy's mom chimed in.

The girls got in formation and stood side by side.

"You can do better than that," said Mr. Johnson. "Show us some moves with . . . 'Style.'" And then, as if on cue, all the parents started embarrassingly singing the song.

The Taylors all pretended to groan this time. Teffy noticed Hannah and Greta watching from the bleachers where they were pulling on sweatpants over their uniforms.

"Stop! Stop!" TS begged. "We'll even do handstands if you stop singing."

"Deal!" said Mrs. Shaw, who had red hair just like her daughter.

They took multiple pictures—arms around one another, posing doing kicks, even a handstand. Each time Teffy smiled so wide her gums were showing for sure, but she didn't care. She was a cheerleader! With all the Taylors! The Bulldogs had won! And they had a sleepover planned again at Tay Tay's that night.

Fifth grade was turning out to be the best year ever.

"I'm so proud of you," Teffy's mom said, coming over to hug her. Her dad did the same. "You looked great out there."

"You think so? We only had two days to get ready for tonight," Teffy said. Her mom gave her a look as if to say, *Don't downplay your success*, which was something she said a lot. "But yeah, it was a lot of fun and we looked pretty good." Her mom touched her forehead to Teffy's.

"That's my girl," her mom said. "As a treat, I told Mr. Johnson I'd send over pizza tonight from Galleria. With breadsticks."

Teffy could almost taste them. The breadsticks were her favorite thing to get at Galleria, but sometimes she felt bad asking for her mom to get them. Pizzas were expensive, and with Charlie eating three slices, they always needed two pies. "Thanks, Mom."

"Have fun, kiddo," Dad said, ruffling her hair.

TS had big goals for them: Tonight they would make one hundred bracelets.

And eat pizza.

"Shotgun!" shouted Tay Tay, jumping into the front passenger seat of her dad's SUV. Mr. Johnson was driving them all to her house. She turned the music up loud and started bouncing in her seat, held back by only her seat belt. "What should we listen to?"

"As if no one knows already," joked Mr. Johnson.

"I'll put it on random." Tay Tay hooked up her phone, which had a clear glitter phone case. "I Can Do It With a Broken Heart" came on as Mr. Johnson joined the throng of cars trying to make their way out of the parking lot. The girls sang along.

Tay Tay put her window down and started singing to the next car—which was a group of teens. She was so brave. Teffy wouldn't have the nerve. Instead, she sang to Taylor and TS, all four of them in the best moods ever.

—•—T-A-Y-L-O-R-S-—•—

"Let the official friendship bracelet session begin!" Tay Tay used her spoon to bang on the metal table in her backyard.

They'd all changed into swimsuits and taken a dip, then chowed down on pizza and were drying off before they started bracelet making. There was still a few more weeks of pool weather coming before fall kicked in. And official fall meant Taylor's Eras Tour stop would be just around the corner. She'd finished her European leg and was headed to Miami in a few weeks. Indianapolis was close behind and the whole city was getting in a Swiftie State of Mind. She heard on the news that some of the streets were going to get new temporary names after Taylor songs, and rumor was, a massive decal of Taylor was going to grace the side of a hotel. The Children's Museum of Indianapolis had just posted about their Swiftie Par-TAY and how they were putting giant friendship bracelets and a big purple microphone on display by their dinosaurs. Teffy felt time rushing by and she hoped they could make their dreams come true. Seeing Taylor together would be something they'd never forget.

"I made thirty-five bracelets since we talked so I feel like if we compete, we might be able to make more," said TS. She shook out her wrist. "I think I have a wrist injury from so much beading." Everyone laughed. "Oh! I also made us those bracelets we talked about." TS ran over to her bag and pulled out four friendship bracelets with the words THE TAYLORS spelled out on them. Each girl put one on.

"I love it!" Teffy gushed. "How do you have time to do all this stuff?"

TS shrugged her freckled shoulders and grinned. "I'm a good multitasker. Ask my mom."

"Let's never take them off," Tay Tay declared, looking at her bracelet from all angles. "We should wear them in the video we're making."

"Yes, and we're making it tonight," Taylor insisted. "We have to put it up on social media ASAP."

"Looking like drowned rats?" Teffy asked, holding up a strand of wet hair. They all laughed.

"We can blow our hair out and put on some makeup too," added Tay Tay. "I have lots."

"Ooh. So fun," TS said. "Half my soccer team wears makeup, but my mom still thinks I'm too young."

"Kid number five," Taylor pointed to herself. "My sister has been practicing makeup on me since I was three. You should see some pictures she has of me with eye shadow on in kindergarten. My mom has one framed in the den."

Teffy loved that Taylor's family was so close. She wished she wasn't always bickering with Charlie. But if she was being honest, she had a feeling they both liked to bug each other sometimes just for the fun of it.

"I can't wear makeup to school," Tay Tay admitted. "But my dad doesn't mind me practicing with it at home." She batted her eyes. "We need stage makeup for our video, darlings!"

I can't wear any makeup, Teffy thought. Her mom had no problem with Teffy buying pretty-smelling moisturizers, but she felt like fifth-grade girls shouldn't wear makeup. Teffy understood, but she also sometimes longed to wear eyeliner like Hannah and look older. Her mom probably would be okay with her putting it on at a sleepover though.

"So we shoot the video and we post it everywhere, and then we wait for Taylor to see it and say, 'What? They're so cute, and such big fans and they deserve tickets to my show'?" TS asked.

Taylor made prayer hands. "That's the hope."

Tay Tay reached for her bead kit and everyone started setting up their supplies. "I forgot to tell you all: I sent a text to all my relatives asking them to try to find us Taylor Swift tickets."

"That's a great idea!" Teffy marveled. "I should do that too. Did your family have any luck?"

"My mom found five the other day on one of the resell sites," TS told them. "They were selling them together for two thousand dollars."

Taylor frowned and began cutting string for her bracelets. "Why didn't you tell us? That's only four hundred dollars a ticket."

TS paused with a bead and string in mid-air. "And?"

"Those were probably the last 'cheap' tickets out there!" Taylor argued. "What if that was our only shot? You should have texted us."

"But we didn't have the money." TS bristled.

Teffy and Tay Tay glanced at each other nervously. The

tension was thick between the girls and Teffy didn't want it blowing up into a fight. "Okay, so let's just agree that any time someone finds what they think are reasonably priced tickets from here on, they tell the group," Teffy suggested.

"Even if we aren't sure if we can afford them," Tay Tay added. "Agreed?"

"Yes," TS and Taylor said glumly, both concentrating on their beading again. TS was quick and almost strung a whole bracelet in under a minute.

"So I learned something cool I wanted to share with the group," Tay Tay said awkwardly, glancing at Teffy again.

"Tell us, Tay Tay!" Teffy said with more enthusiasm than necessary. A subject change was a good idea!

Tay Tay grinned. "My cousin Leyna told me she goes to a zillion concerts and she gets her tickets from social media posts."

"Really? How?" TS asked as she sorted bead colors.

"She said Swifties want to help fellow Swifties, so if they post about having extra tickets, and they're willing to send a video of the tickets on Ticketmaster and their actual screen, then we will know they're not fake."

"Yeah, but we still have to be able to afford the tickets," Taylor reminded her. "And I'm sure even Swifties won't offer them for four hundred dollars again."

TS shot her a look. "Miracles happen!"

Uh-oh, Teffy thought. "Hey!" she said extra loud. "I forgot to tell you all: I sold out of Harrison bracelets at the game today and we made twenty bucks."

"So with all our pooled birthday money, and money from the bracelets, plus the four hundred we are getting for making the sweet sixteen bracelets, we have six hundred and twenty dollars," Tay Tay calculated. "That's pretty good."

"But not enough," Taylor pointed out again, all doom and gloom.

Teffy wanted to throw a pool float at her. "But if we finish all the sweet sixteen bracelets tonight, we can start on *more* Harrison bracelets. And Mr. Ball put in an order for five and Ms. Cherie requested two for her nieces. So that's more orders."

Taylor leaned her head on Teffy, her wet, dark hair spilling onto her. "You're right. Sorry I'm a grouch." She smiled apologetically at TS. "Six hundred is great."

Just then they heard a phone ring. It was TS's. "It's my grandma. I have to get it. Hi, Grandma," TS said, and paused, listening. TS's blue eyes widened. "Wait. Really? Really, really, really?" Her voice shot up. "Are you sure?" She looked at the other Taylors.

"What is it?" Teffy whispered. Did they get tickets?

TS covered her phone with her hand. "My grandmother said her senior center is raffling off two tickets and she can buy all the raffle tickets we want to try to win them for us."

"But they only have two?" Tay Tay reminded her gently.

TS's face fell. "Right. Should we try to get them and resell them to buy our own tickets?"

"No," Taylor said, threading beads. "We just said Swifties wouldn't jack ticket prices up and we are Swifties. If we win tickets and do that to some other fan, it feels wrong."

"You're right," TS said, her brow furrowing. She took her hand off the phone. "Grandma? Thank you, but it's okay. We need five tickets." She listened for a moment and smiled. "Yes. Five or none of us are going. Okay. You work your magic. Love you!" TS hung up and looked at them. "She said she'd try to get the senior center to find more tickets so she can win us five."

"I love an ambitious grandma," Tay Tay said as she cut another piece of string.

"My sister said we should also try writing to some radio stations and share how we are named after Taylor and want to go together," said TS. "Maybe someone will want to help us."

Teffy nodded. "It can't hurt."

Tay Tay grinned and bounced in her chair as "22" came on. "Chin up, people!" She grabbed her bead box and started threading. "Our ticket plans are just getting started."

FOURTEEN

long story short

September flew by, filled with both highs and lows. (Teffy's parents loved playing that game with her and Charlie at dinner: "What's your high from today? What's your low? What's your buffalo? Ha!")

Highs: They cheered at three Bulldogs home games and Halloween was around the corner. Teffy loved the Taylors' group costume idea: Each Taylor was going as a different album cover look.

Taylor was going as *Lover*. She was wearing a pink boa, a shimmery mermaid-style dress, and some booties that were her sister's.

Teffy was channeling *folklore* with a white button-down shirt with a collar, and a plaid tan dress that looked similar to something Teffy could picture Taylor wearing in everyday life. The songwriting on *folklore* was some of her favorite, and she wanted to represent it.

Tay Tay was going with a *Fearless* album look complete with a sparkly silver flapper dress.

And TS had lobbied hard for *Red* and went with a "22" look—heart-shaped red sunglasses, a black fedora hat, black shorts, and a 22 tee.

September Lows: The Harrison Library had an electrical fire and was so badly damaged it had to close indefinitely. The repairs needed were extensive on the historical building, which had been built in 1898, and it would take a lot of money to reopen. Teffy was devastated. She visited the library almost weekly to keep up with her book habit.

A buffalo (which was sort of also a high): In school, Mr. Ball decided they were ready for their first small-group assignment—Read and Rap. Liam had told her Mr. Ball's Read and Rap project was legendary—kids either absolutely loved it because they got the best team or they hated it because one person was stuck doing all the reading *and* all the planning for the presentation. They'd have four weeks to read their book and come up with their assignment. Then, during the last week of October, they'd perform their scenes in front of the class.

"Basically, I will divide you into groups of four and I want you all to read a book together, discuss it, and then perform a scene from the book for the class," Mr. Ball explained. "It doesn't have to be a rap, but if you want to channel your inner Lin-Manuel Miranda, I'm all for it. You can act it out, do choreography, mime, sing—the more creative, the higher the score." He grinned. "I'm a musical fan so do not fear doing something big and bold."

There was nervous laughter around the room. Teffy picked at her nails and tried to control her breathing. Acting? Miming? None of this was in her comfort zone, but she was a cheerleader now. She'd started to be bolder, cheering loudly. Maybe she could do this too. The Taylors' eyes found one another—Mr. Ball had changed everyone's seat assignments three times already (his pattern seemed to be every two weeks). Would any of them be together? They never got in trouble for talking while he was teaching and none of them passed notes, so maybe. He liked that the girls were all friends and shared nicknames.

"When I call your name, please stand and move to the front of the room to meet your Rap-Mates," said Mr. Ball. "You see what I did there?" The class groaned good-naturedly.

Teffy placed her hands under her butt and waited anxiously to hear her name called. The "picking a book" part was going to be fun. She was thinking *Faker* by Gordon Korman or maybe something fairy tale like Jennifer A. Nielsen's *The False Prince*. Though a person couldn't go wrong with *Witchlings* by Claribel A. Ortega.

"Teffy Bennett, come on down!" Mr. Ball said in a game show voice. People applauded. "Let's get Tay Tay Johnson and Akif Darwish too!"

Yes, Teffy thought. She was with Tay Tay! The two girls hugged as they met in the front of the room.

"And last, but not least, let's get Hannah Reed up here."

Hannah? Teffy felt her stomach clench.

Hannah gave Akif and Tay Tay high fives, turning to ask Mr. Ball a question so she wouldn't have to give Teffy one. Teffy resisted the urge to roll her eyes. She didn't get why Hannah was so rude to her but tried her hardest to talk to Taylor or TS. Maybe it was because their sisters knew each other. Strangely, when Ms. Cherie tried to take a picture of the Taylors yesterday, Hannah and Greta jumped in. Why would they want to be in their picture when they didn't want Tay Tay and Teffy at their lunch table? It didn't make sense.

Teffy would just make the best of this Read and Rap assignment. She was being brave now, after all.

Today Hannah had on one of those expensive tees from a company in Australia that all the girls were obsessed with. Teffy put one of their shirts on her birthday list, but her birthday wasn't till January, so it was going to be a while. Hannah had three shirts. This one was pink. *Someone is always going to have more than you and someone is always going to have less*, she could hear her mom saying. Her mom was right. Hannah was her teammate—both in cheer and on this project. They needed to learn to coexist.

"Hey, Hannah," Teffy tried.

Hannah glanced at her briefly. "Hey." Hannah headed to the back table in the classroom their team was assigned to. Tay Tay and Akif took seats next to Teffy and Hannah on the special squishy chairs everyone loved.

"Let's pick a book," said Akif. "Anyone have any suggestions?"

"Something fun so we can have the best performance. I'm meant to be onstage." Tay Tay stood up and theatrically took a bow.

"I hate reading," said Hannah, tapping her pencil. "Someone else pick."

No one wonder we don't get along, Teffy thought. "I have some suggestions," she said. "*Witchlings* by Claribel A. Ortega is about witches our age, and it's a fun adventure. Whatever After by Sarah Mlynowski is a fairy-tale mashup series I love, and there's also *The Liars Society* by Alyson Gerber, which has a secret school society in it that's very cool."

Hannah just looked at her. "How do you know all that?"

"Teffy keeps a list of books she reads, and she's read over a hundred books this year already," Tay Tay said as she pulled her hair into a knot and tied it with a pencil. Teffy smiled at her friend gratefully.

"Because all she does is read." Hannah sniffed. "I have dance class four days a week after cheerleading. And homework. I'm not just up in my room reading a boring book."

"These books aren't boring," Teffy said, proud of herself for opening her mouth.

Hannah just shrugged. "Just pick one then. I don't care. As long as it's not long."

Tay Tay and Akif both seemed to be waiting for Teffy to make a decision too.

"Well, it is almost Halloween, so let's go with *Witchlings*," Teffy suggested. "Witches fit with the theme."

"Ooh!" Tay Tay slammed her hands dramatically on the table. "What if we did a cheer based on the book that tells the story?" Tay Tay smiled at her. "Teffy loves to write songs. I bet she could come up with a good one."

"I'm in," said Akif.

They all turned to Hannah, who was fidgeting on the squishy chair. "Fine. I guess so." She looked at Teffy. "But your cheer better be good."

Teffy loved a challenge. "It will be."

FIFTEEN

Don't Blame Me

One week into the project, and Teffy had to admit: She was enjoying it. Especially the "reading something fun" part. *Witchlings* was good. Now they just had to make sure the cheer they performed was as well.

"Okay, we should all be almost halfway through the book," Tay Tay told the team as they gathered at a table in the back of the room. "I feel like we have to pick a scene for Teffy to use for the cheer at this point, no?"

Akif frowned. "You're only halfway through? I finished two nights ago."

"You finished?" Hannah's nostrils flared. "It's only been a week! And the school library only got our copies in four days ago."

"I did too." Teffy tried not to sound braggy. This was the second time she was reading the book, but she didn't mention that part. Hannah gave her a look. "I'm a fast reader."

"Well, I'm not." Hannah sounded mad at Teffy about that fact.

"Maybe you're distracted," Akif said, spinning his pencil on the table. "Do you have your phone in the room when you're doing homework? I'm not allowed to look at social media on school nights."

I'm not allowed social media at all, Teffy thought.

"So I guess you didn't see the Taylors' video begging to get Taylor tickets," Hannah said mockingly as she gave Teffy a snide smile. Akif looked confused.

"You have to watch," Tay Tay said, missing Hannah's sarcasm. "The video has over a thousand views and three hundred likes."

Hannah played with the glitter star eraser in her hand. "Only three hundred likes? My friends and I make videos together all the time and our videos get, like, a thousand likes."

She's lying, Teffy thought.

Tay Tay frowned. "A thousand likes? Really?"

"Yes," Hannah insisted. "My posts are public. Plus, all my sister's friends follow me and they're in high school."

In her head, Teffy rolled her eyes.

"Taylor posted this one and she's public so hopefully it gets thousands of likes too." Tay Tay sighed blissfully and doodled a picture of a microphone in her notebook. Hannah never soured her mood. "And then Taylor Swift herself will comment and give us tickets. That's what we're hoping."

Hannah snorted. "Keep dreaming." She turned to Teffy. "How many followers do you have?"

A million answers went through Teffy's mind in seconds.

"Oh, Teffy doesn't have a phone yet," Tay Tay jumped in without thinking. "She's not allowed social media." Tay Tay froze and it was clear she realized her mistake, but the damage was already done.

"Pfft!" Hannah started to laugh. "You don't even have *a phone*?"

Teffy felt her face burn. She tried to think of something witty to say—like Tay Tay had done earlier—but her mind was blank. She wished the floor would swallow her up whole. The Taylors knew she didn't have a phone, but it kind of went without saying that Teffy wasn't screaming the news from the school bleachers on a megaphone. She didn't want the whole school to know she was the girl without a phone.

Akif looked intrigued rather than judgy. "So how do you reach your mom if you have something after school and it runs late? Or you forget your lunch, which I have done at least three times already."

"It's not a big deal," Tay Tay said, her voice extra loud and nervous as she tried to smooth things over. "Teffy can still text from her iPad and Xbox, right, Teffy?"

"I . . ." Teffy's heart started to beat faster and she tried to stay calm, but the situation kept getting worse.

"Her Xbox?" Hannah repeated. She pulled on Greta's arm at the table behind them. "Greta, guess what? Teffy doesn't have a phone!"

Greta's eyes widened and she looked at Teffy. "You don't have a phone?"

"Who doesn't have a phone?" asked Max from Greta's group.

"Teffy," Greta repeated.

She could feel her heart pounding in her chest. *Think, Teffy*, she told herself. *Say something funny. Make a joke about it.* But instead, Hannah spoke first.

"Aww . . . poor Teffy! You must be the only person at Harrison Middle School without a phone." Hannah was smiling with her teeth, as if she were trying to be funny, but she looked kind of scary.

Teffy blinked back tears. Everyone would be talking about this at lunch. And on the school bus. And at cheer practice. She was going to be the one girl alive who had no cell phone. *Hold it together*, she told herself. She pushed her chair back and heard it scrape against the floor.

"Teffy, wait!" Tay Tay called as she rushed up to Mr. Ball's desk. The other Taylors were looking up now too.

"Can I go to the bathroom?" Teffy asked Mr. Ball.

"Of course. Take the pass." He pointed to the hook on the wall, where a wooden plank with a bulldog etched onto it served as the hall pass. She could hear Hannah laughing.

"Are you okay?" TS frowned as Teffy blew past her. "Teffy?"

But Teffy didn't want to talk to anyone. She pushed her way out of the classroom and hurried down the fifth-grade hall, counting the steps till she got to the bathroom.

She was so mad.

At her mom and dad for believing fifth graders didn't need phones.

At herself for not having a comeback ready to clap back at Hannah.

At Tay Tay for spilling the beans.

At Hannah, who would never let her live this down.

Teffy heard the bell ring.

Lunch period was next.

Great.

Even though she wasn't at Hannah's lunch table, this was all anyone was going to talk about. She barely reached the bathroom doors before other classroom doors started opening. Fearful someone would be coming in right behind her, she ducked into the first stall and locked the door. Leaning her head against the wall, she let the tears come, trying to cry as quietly as she could. People didn't cry in the fifth grade, did they?

She heard the door creak open.

"Teffy?" It was Tay Tay. " I'm so sorry." Teffy didn't answer. She didn't want the Taylors to see her crying. "I feel so bad. Please come out and be mad at me."

"We know you're in here," said Taylor, pounding on bathroom stalls.

Teffy still didn't say anything. If she'd been smarter, she'd have stepped onto the toilet to hide herself. But that sounded kind of gross. A sob escaped her lips, giving her away.

"Teffy, please?" TS begged. "Don't be embarrassed. You're not the only one without a phone. Hannah is mean. Come out so I can give you a hug."

Teffy tried to calm down but that only made her cry harder.

"We can see your sneakers," Taylor said, beginning to sound impatient.

"Please let me apologize." Tay Tay sounded upset now too. "I'm an Aimee."

"You're definitely an Aimee," Taylor and TS said at the same time.

A laugh escaped Teffy's throat. Tay Tay was not an Aimee. She'd made a mistake. A mistake that embarrassed her, but Teffy knew deep down Tay Tay didn't do it on purpose. Slowly, she opened the bathroom stall. Her friends saw her tear-stained face and theirs fell. Tay Tay ran for Teffy, squeezing her so hard it hurt.

"I'm so sorry," Tay Tay said. "I wasn't thinking!"

"I know," said Teffy. "I'm sorry I got so upset." She placed her head in her hands. "Not having a phone is just embarrassing and Hannah is never going to let me live it down." She wiped her eyes with the back of her sleeve. "See? *I cry a lot, but I am so productive.*"

"Stop crying. Who cares what Hannah thinks?" TS threw up her hands, her friendship bracelets sliding down her arms. Today she was wearing a purple tee that had a picture of a snowman on it and said CHILL OUT. "Do you think I care when someone makes fun of my lunch box? Or my weird T-shirts?" She shrugged. "Those things are what make me 'me.'" She grinned. "You need to learn to live alongside cringe."

Teffy's brow furrowed. "What do you mean?"

"Yeah, what even is cringe?" Tay Tay asked. "Is that another word for cat lovers?"

"No!" TS laughed. "It means love yourself. Have fun. Don't be afraid to be who you are. So what, you don't have a phone yet? Own it."

Own it. Be more confident. Find your voice. Isn't that what Teffy was trying to do this year? How had she let Hannah's dig make her forget that? So what that she didn't have a phone? She had done so much in fifth grade already. Made a friend group, started a small bracelet-making business. She was a cheerleader! "How did you get so wise?"

"I didn't," TS said. "I stole that line from Mother." The other Taylors looked confused. "I mean Taylor. As in Swift?"

"Ohhhhh." It took them all a minute.

"The cringe thing is something Taylor said in that commencement speech she gave at NYU." TS looked around the bathroom at their blank faces and her voice echoed. "None of you have seen the video? Read the speech?" The other Taylors shook their heads. "Okay, I'm giving you all homework. I'll send you a link after school. Teffy, you can read it on your iPad and be proud."

The girls all started to giggle, Teffy included.

"Yes, Professor Shaw," Teffy teased. She looked around at her friends. "Thanks for coming to find me in the bathroom."

Tay Tay lunged forward and bear-hugged her again. "I'm sorry! I just need to say it this last time and I'll stop apologizing. I promise."

"I know." Teffy let Tay Tay hug her till she was ready to let go. "Forget it. It's over." She sighed. "I still wish I had a better comeback for Hannah. I shut down when she started with me."

"Hannah is a mean girl," Tay Tay declared.

"Sometimes," Taylor interjected. The other girls looked at her. "When she came over to my house last weekend with her sister to hang out—"

"Wait. You hung out with Hannah?" TS said accusingly.

"It wasn't planned. She came over with her sister and she wasn't completely awful," Taylor said uncomfortably. "But, Teffy, I swear. If she makes you feel bad again, I will go full *Reputation* on her and throw down!"

Teffy laughed. "Thanks. I just wish I knew how to handle Hannah. I never know what to say."

"You start by saying *something*," Taylor said sharply. "Use your voice. Just like you do in cheer. She can't make you feel bad if you don't let her."

Teffy nodded. Taylor was blunt, but she was rarely wrong at understanding a situation. "You're right. You all are." She glanced at TS. "I should embrace the cringe, but also use my voice."

Tay Tay grinned. "Taylors for life?"

Teffy smiled. "Taylors for life," she agreed.

SIXTEEN

I Knew You Were Trouble

"We are Harrison and we're here to say, 'We are going to make your day!'

"Will we let you win? We say, 'No way!'

"But we'll smile and cheer, and you'll have a good time anyway!

"Go Harrison!"

From the sidelines of Harrison Middle School, the fifth- and sixth-grade cheer squad stood in the sunshine and belted out their cheers. The Taylors were particularly happy for more reasons than one.

After several weeks of rain, the sun was back.

So was Tay Tay, who had missed almost a week of school and had to cancel their last sleepover and bracelet-making session when she got a virus.

But now everyone was healthy and ready for Halloween, the

Eras Tour was stateside again, which meant Taylor's concerts in Indianapolis were a week away, and today the Bulldogs had Homecoming.

Homecoming was a big deal at Harrison Middle School. There were food trucks, balloons, and it felt like everyone in attendance had school spirit. The stands were packed with people wearing navy and white. Teffy could see her parents front and center. Her dad had made a tiny cardboard cutout with the Taylors' group picture on it and was waving it like a pom-pom.

Ms. Cherie had told the Taylors they could sell friendship bracelets at the high school game the night before, and before and after this game, and they'd done well. They'd already sold fifty bracelets! That was another hundred bucks. Plus, some girl's mom put in an order for twenty-five bracelets so that her daughter didn't have to make her own to bring to the Taylor concert next Saturday. Another mom heard and said she wanted to place an order too. Teffy's head was spinning. If her math was correct, between all the new orders and the sales this past week, they had over a thousand dollars now!

Maybe they could make more this week. A lot more. Teffy tried to focus on the cheer, but inside she was thinking about what would happen if her mom put a post on social media about the girls making friendship bracelets for the concert. Other busy moms might want them too.

Could they make the fifty bracelets already ordered this week plus two hundred more? Which would be another four hundred dollars, which would bring their total to almost fifteen hundred dollars?

God, she hated math.

But if her calculations were right, maybe that number would bring them close enough to buy last-minute seats. They could use Tay Tay's method to find someone legit selling them online.

Inwardly, Teffy screamed with excitement. She couldn't wait to tell the others.

The game buzzer sounded and there was a loud cheer, pulling her from her thoughts.

"The Bulldogs have won it again, 27–7!" said the announcer from the booth above the bleachers. The cheerleaders waved their pom-poms and did their best high kicks.

Ms. Cherie came over to the squad. "Girls, that was amazing! You looked great out there!" She eyed Teffy. "And can we all give a huge, round-the-world clap for Teffy, who wrote today's stellar new cheer?" Ms. Cherie smiled. "I can't wait to see what else you come up with."

Teffy couldn't hide her pride as everyone around her applauded and shouted her name.

They'd been practicing several of Teffy's cheers at practice, but hadn't ended up using one in a game till now. This new cheer had come to Teffy when she was in her room last week trying to write the cheer they were using for their Read and Rap project about *Witchlings*. They'd picked the moment when one of the characters finds out that if she fails her quest, she could wind up becoming a toad. Teffy's favorite line in the cheer so far was "Who needs a coven when you've got us? Spares ready to stop a friendship apocalypse!" She had a feeling Mr. Ball would like that she was using a word as big as *apocalypse* in their project. She'd been so inspired, she'd worked on a Bulldogs cheer too and sent it to Ms. Cherie. Ms. Cherie taught the girls the cheer at the next practice but hadn't said where it came from till now. Teffy was grinning ear to ear.

"That's our Teffy!" Tay Tay threw her arms around her, and TS and Taylor piled on.

Out of the corner of her eye, Teffy could swear she saw

Hannah brooding. Hannah had only made one other comment since the phone "incident," and since it was done under her breath, Teffy didn't respond. But she was ready. She'd been practicing things to say if Hannah started with her in her mirror.

"We still have two more home games, but next weekend we have a bye week, which means you're off," Ms. Cherie told the squad. "So for those of you going to the Eras Tour, you can tailgate at dawn." Everyone laughed. "For the rest of you, the good news is I'm giving you Halloween off too. Enjoy!"

As everyone walked to the bleachers to get their things, Teffy noticed Hannah with Taylor. The two were whispering heatedly and Teffy wondered what was going on. Were they fighting about something? Taylor would probably tell her later. Right now, they had bracelets to sell.

Teffy grabbed her bag and rushed to the Bulldogs merchandise tent. Older cheerleaders were already there handling snack sales and merchandise.

"Teffy!" Paola, one of the eighth-grade cheerleaders, waved to her. "You've already got a line."

"A line?" Teffy gaped when she saw all the moms and kids standing behind the bracelet sign the Taylors had made.

"Whoa!" TS skidded to a stop next to her. "That's for us?"

"It is for us!" said Tay Tay, approaching now too.

"Let's get over there!" TS declared, rushing into the booth. In seconds, they had a system—TS taking orders, Tay Tay taking money, Teffy doing the selling and showing off of different designs. Today, they were selling an array of designs: Harrison and Bulldogs bracelets, and ones for Swifties. Those were the biggest sellers.

A mom in line with her twin daughters stepped up to the counter. "Do you have any that say 'Swiftie' that look *exactly* the same? Bead for bead?" She looked at her girls warily. "I need them to be identical."

"I don't today, but I could have them ready for you on Monday if you write down your phone number." Teffy passed her a pad of paper where they were taking additional orders.

TS tapped her arm. "We actually need ten identical Swiftie bracelets over here."

"And I just got an order for ten more over here," Tay Tay called out, and waved her pom-poms in the air in celebration.

Teffy tried to do the math in her head: They had fifty orders before this, now another twenty-two and . . . grr! Mr. Ball was right. Math was important. They needed help here. She whirled around. "Hey. Where is Taylor?"

Tay Tay shrugged. "Don't know. I saw her arguing with Hannah earlier."

"What were they fighting about?" Teffy asked.

TS shook her head. "Not a clue. Probably Hannah being Hannah."

It felt like Hannah was trying to steal Taylor away from the group more and more lately. Teffy knew Taylor's and Hannah's sisters were good friends, but it also felt like Hannah loved separating the Taylors. Teffy knew Hannah and Taylor had hung out before, but were they friends too? Had they hung out more than once? If they had, did it matter? The Taylors were allowed to have other friends too. Yes, Teffy sounded jealous and she knew it, but there was something about Hannah whispering to Taylor earlier that was strange. "I hope she hurries. We're swamped." Teffy started counting heads in line. "I wonder how many people here are looking for bracelets for the Eras Tour. We should keep a list."

"Let's find out." Tay Tay cupped her hands over her mouth. "Everyone looking to buy friendship bracelets for the Eras Tour, raise your hand!"

Every person in line raised their hand.

TS squealed. "You know what this means?"

"I'm afraid to say it out loud." Teffy's heart was pounding. "If we can get all these bracelets done in time, we're going to have a lot more money to buy tickets."

"We can get it done if we stay up all night beading bracelets at my house," Tay Tay said with a grin.

"I'm sure my mom will say yes," Teffy said. "I'm in."

"Me too!" TS was still selling whatever bracelets they had left. "I will make three times the amount any of you make," she vowed, and they laughed. "I should text my mom to start looking for tickets again."

Teffy had goose bumps. The Taylors had money to search for tickets! They still had a shot! She was practically floating for the next hour as they worked the booth. They sold out of everything they had—even the Bulldogs bracelets. It only occurred to Teffy as they were cleaning up that Taylor hadn't shown up to help them. As they were leaving, they spotted her walking toward them. Taylor was wearing a baggy Bulldogs sweatshirt over her cheer uniform. She looked ill.

"Hey! Are you okay?" Teffy asked, concerned.

"Where were you?" Tay Tay asked. "We sold out of our bracelets!"

"Huge news: We might have over two thousand dollars if we get our new orders done in time," TS told her. "You know what that means? We can probably buy tickets to the concert!"

Tay Tay did the running man and TS busted out some dance moves. Teffy was giddy.

The only one who didn't look excited was Taylor.

"Two thousand dollars is not enough money," she said, not making eye contact. "My mom looked last night, and people are selling seats for fifteen hundred a piece now."

"Fifteen hundred?" Teffy deflated. If that was true, even with all the new orders, they wouldn't have enough.

"Prices are going up every day! We're never going to make enough money to go together!" Taylor looked like she was on the verge of tears.

The Taylors looked at one another in alarm.

TS reached out and touched Taylor's arm. "Hey. What's wrong?"

Taylor shook her head and stepped away, wrapping her arms

around herself. She wouldn't make eye contact. "I have to tell you all something."

Teffy had a bad feeling. Her stomach started to twist.

"What is it?" Tay Tay whispered, and she reached for TS's hand.

A group of the sixth-grade football players walked by, including Liam, who waved. Teffy waved back, but her heart was pounding now. Why was Taylor being so weird?

"Last weekend when Tay Tay was sick, Hannah and her sister came over to my house to hang out again and Hannah asked me to go to the Eras show with her." Taylor said the words really fast, still not looking at them. "Her sister asked my sister too so it would be the four of us and her parents." She swallowed hard. "I didn't give her an answer at first, but I just said yes."

Teffy felt a whistling sound in her ears. "But. . . . we made a pact."

Taylor looked up, her eyes brimming with tears. "It was a ridiculous pact. We were never going to get five tickets. And we were never going to have enough money for them even if we found tickets!"

"So you're taking Hannah's freebie ticket and going without

us?" Tay Tay said, getting mad now, angry tears springing to her eyes. "My dad could have gotten two tickets, but I said no."

"Me too!" said TS, upset as well. "My grandma had that raffle we could have won!"

Teffy's heart was pounding. "We said if we couldn't get tickets together, then no one was going and we were going to tailgate together."

Taylor shifted uncomfortably. "I know, but . . . my sister . . ." She paused. "Look, I already said yes. I can't change my mind and back out now. I just wanted you all to know."

Teffy couldn't believe what she was hearing. Did Taylor expect them to be okay with this? That she was going with Hannah after they'd all agreed to go together or not at all? *Hannah?* The girl who tormented Teffy about cheer, about not having a phone? It was bad enough that Taylor hung out with Hannah anyway. Now they were going to the Eras Tour together? No. This was wrong.

She felt an uncomfortable sensation rumbling up deep from inside her. The old Teffy would have just accepted it and stewed in silence. But hadn't Taylor been the one to tell her to speak up and use her voice?

"You're a bad friend!" Teffy snapped, tears streaming down

her face as Tay Tay and TS looked on in surprise. "I can't believe you're going with Hannah after we made a pact!"

Taylor pursed her lips. "It was a stupid idea. We were never going to get tickets."

"No, what's stupid is us thinking you were our friend." Taylor's eyes widened in surprise as Teffy folded her arms over her chest to keep from shaking. "You know what? If you're going to the concert with Hannah, then maybe you should trick-or-treat with her too!"

"Maybe we all should—" Tay Tay started to say. Taylor cut her off.

"Fine! If you're going to be like that, I don't want to go with you anyway."

"Good!" Teffy kept going, charged up now. "Because it's Hannah or us. Not just for trick-or-treating!" She was on a roll now and couldn't stop herself. "You have to decide: Who do you want to be friends with, us or Hannah? You can't have us both."

Taylor's eyes widened in surprise then narrowed. "I . . ."

"Er . . . Teffy," TS tried to intervene.

"Pick one!" Teffy yelled.

Taylor stood there, stunned. It was the first time Teffy could remember Taylor not having a quip or a comeback.

Teffy's tears were hot as they spilled down her cheeks. The words she said next were ones she knew she couldn't take back. But she didn't care. "Fine. We'll decide for you. You're no longer one of the Taylors."

"Teffy!" Tay Tay hissed.

"I don't want to be a Taylor anyway!" Taylor said, shaking.

"Wait!" TS tried, even though she was crying too. "Can we at least talk about this?"

"No. I don't ever want to talk to any of you ever again," said Taylor, pushing her way past them, leaving the other three Taylors standing in her wake.

SEVENTEEN

exile

For the first time since the year started, Teffy dreaded going to school.

If her group wasn't supposed to do their Read and Rap presentation, Teffy would have begged her mom to let her take a sick day. She certainly felt sick—she didn't have an appetite, her stomach hurt, and she couldn't stop crying. She was exhausted from fighting with Taylor, and she didn't want to talk to anyone, not even the other Taylors.

After the fight, they'd decided to cancel the sleepover and all go home. No one had spoken since. Her iPad was silent all weekend. None of the girls texted either. Were Tay Tay and TS mad at her too? Taylor was wrong for what she did, but Teffy felt awful about what she'd said to her. Who was she to decide Taylor could no longer be one of the Taylors? Was what she did any different from Hannah kicking her and Tay Tay off their lunch table?

She wished she could take the fight back and start over.

Walking down the hall to Mr. Ball's class, Teffy spotted TS and Tay Tay talking. They saw her and stopped. Teffy felt her stomach start to swirl with nerves as she approached her friends. "Hey."

"Hey," they said, not making eye contact.

They're definitely mad at me. Teffy wasn't sure what to say. "I finished two of the moms' bracelet orders and made twenty-five Eras Tour ones." She felt her face burn. "I had lots of time this weekend." *I'm sorry for the fight*, she wanted to say. Suddenly, she couldn't find her voice again.

"I made a hundred," TS said, still competitive but not sounding like she was bragging. "I don't know if we need that many. Or if it even matters now . . ." She bit the inside of her cheek.

"We were just talking about tickets," Tay Tay told Teffy. She wasn't her usual bubbly self. "Taylor is right. The prices keep going up. They're selling for two or three thousand dollars each now."

Teffy almost choked. "Each?"

Tay Tay pulled at the sleeve of her aqua top, which she seemed to be stretching out. "It's less than a week till the first show.

There was nothing under that price except one listing and my dad said it was probably a bot trying to scam us and—" Tay Tay stiffened.

Taylor walked by the group fast, not looking over.

Teffy felt queasy and her jaw locked as she stared at their friend trying to avoid them. Teffy didn't know what to do. Did she say something? She didn't want to. Just seeing Taylor again made her mad. And sad. Mad and sad. It wasn't a good combo.

"Taylor! Wait up!"

Teffy's stomach rolled at the sound of Hannah's voice. Hannah was running toward Taylor. Today, she was wearing a T-shirt that said BUT DADDY I LOVE HIM with leggings. She smirked when she saw the Taylors watching.

"Five days till we go to the Eras Tour! Woot! Woot!" Hannah said, fist-pumping the air as she tried to catch Taylor, who raced into the classroom without her.

Behind them, they heard a choked sob. Greta rushed by, head down, sniffling. Teffy had almost forgotten how badly Greta wanted to be Hannah's plus-one for the show. She'd overheard Greta tell someone she was already planning her outfit.

It felt like no one was having a good day.

Tay Tay sighed loudly. "I think we have to face facts: Our Eras Tour dream is over."

"It was a nice dream while it lasted," TS said quietly, admitting defeat too, which was not like her at all.

"My mom said she'd still take us Tay-Gating," Teffy said miserably, and looked down at her TAYLORS friendship bracelet. Fight or no fight, she couldn't take it off. She noticed Tay Tay and TS had theirs on too. "She heard they're not opening the dome for the concert, but there will still be parking lots nearby doing bracelet trading and listening parties."

Neither TS nor Tay Tay said anything. Maybe they didn't want to go with her now. Teffy felt like she was going to cry again. None of the Taylors were acting like themselves, including her. "I'm sorry about the fight," she finally blurted out, and the girls looked at her. "I shouldn't have told Taylor she can't trick-or-treat with us. I should have asked you first."

TS bit her lip. "You were mad. We all were."

Tay Tay nodded. "And we still are mad too, but . . ." She made eye contact with Teffy now. "Friends don't talk for their friends. You should have let us tell Taylor how we felt too."

Here it comes: We don't want to be friends with you anymore, Teffy imagined Tay Tay telling her. "You're right. I'm sorry I did that." She blinked back tears. "If you don't want to be my friend anymore, I understand."

"Don't be ridiculous!" Tay Tay pulled Teffy to her side. "We still love you."

"Friends also forgive each other," TS said. "We all screw up sometimes."

"Remember me blabbing about you not having a phone?" Tay Tay reminded her (as if she needed reminding). "We just wanted you to know how we felt."

Teffy might cry anyway just because she was happy. Her friends had forgiven her. "I'm glad you told me. I really am sorry. I was just hurt, and Taylor kept telling me to use my voice so I did."

"You sure did!" Tay Tay said, and they all sort of laughed. Her face fell. "Besides, Taylor deserved it."

"But . . ." TS said, hesitating.

"We still miss her," Teffy realized, and as she looked at her friends, she knew they felt the same way. "So what do we do now?"

Halloween was days away and they'd been planning their outfits for weeks. Taylor was the one who suggested whatever

Taylor Swift era they dressed as for Halloween should be the outfit they wear to the concert and they'd all agreed.

Now with Taylor gone, they'd be missing the *Lover* era.

But what really mattered was they were missing Taylor.

Because as mad as Teffy was, she had a feeling TS and Tay Tay missed Taylor as much as she did. It was like having a PB and J sandwich without the J. Mac and cheese without the cheese. A Taylor Swift Eras Tour concert without someone getting the hat.

The Taylors didn't work unless it was the four of them.

The bell rang before anyone had the chance to answer Teffy's question.

Now it was time to face Taylor in class. The Taylors presented a united front as they walked in the classroom and took their seats on opposite sides of the room. Teffy's heart was in her throat as she glanced at Taylor. Their friend had her head down as Mr. Ball did roll call. Then it was morning announcements, and home-work review. Finally, it was time for Read and Rap performances, and as luck would have it, Teffy's group was up first.

"Could Tay Tay, Teffy, Hannah, and Akif come up for their performance of *Witchlings*?" Mr. Ball asked.

Teffy felt more nervous than she had at cheer auditions as she walked up to the front of the room. Akif was doing stretches as if he was preparing to do high kicks during their cheer. Hannah looked smug. Teffy took a deep breath and walked up to her Rap-Mates. "Here," she said, handing them purple flash cards. "I made copies of the cheer for everyone so we don't forget our lines."

"Nice!" said Akif, swiping one. "I wrote the cheer on my arm, but it washed off in the shower."

"I'll take one," said Tay Tay.

"I don't need a flash card," Hannah said snippily. "The cheer you wrote is so boring, I memorized it in seconds."

Teffy saw Taylor glance her way from her seat and Teffy knew what she had to do: Use her voice. "If you thought my cheer was that boring, then why didn't you come up with a single line for our cheer yourself?" Teffy asked. Hannah looked stunned and shut her mouth. Tay Tay grinned. At her seat, Teffy saw Taylor bite back a smile.

Yesssss, Teffy thought, and as they got in line to perform, Teffy couldn't help but smile as she noticed something even better: Taylor was still wearing her TAYLORS bracelet too.

EIGHTEEN

Bad Blood

"Boo!" Charlie screamed, jumping into Teffy's doorway. He was wearing zombie makeup, and had on old jeans and a tee shredded and dyed with fake blood. He was also sporting vampire teeth.

"You do know zombies and vampires aren't the same thing, don't you?" Teffy asked.

"Alex and I decided we are zom-pires. Get it? Zombie-vampires?" Charlie smiled brightly, his glow-in-the-dark vampire teeth on full display.

"That's ridiculous," Teffy said and turned back to her bedroom mirror.

Charlie sighed extra loud. "You're just cranky because the Taylors broke up." He walked out of the room again.

"We did not break up!" Teffy yelled, then looked at her Taylor concert photo on her mirror. She'd updated it since the summer and this one was of Taylor spinning in a beautiful white dress. "I think."

Teffy looked at the sleeves of the white shirt her mom had gotten her to match her *folklore* era look. She'd paired it with a tan plaid dress that felt very Taylor. Teffy wrapped her arms around herself. She still felt so down about the fight with Taylor, she was too upset to eat any of the Halloween candy her mom had bought. Even getting an A on the Read and Rap project didn't cheer her up. Teffy knew she and Tay Tay hadn't given the cheer their all. It was clear they were all upset about the fight. Teffy just didn't know how to fix things. Taylor had been sitting at Hannah's lunch table all week while Greta sat at theirs, and after school they had cheer practice and Hannah was always talking to Taylor then too.

"What do I do?" Teffy asked the Taylor picture on her mirror. Next to it was a picture of the Taylors at their first football game. And above that was their list of ways they were going to try to get Eras concert tickets. "I was really liking middle school and fifth grade before the fight with Taylor," Teffy whispered. "I've never had friends this fun before. Who I did everything with. But now nothing feels right. What Taylor did was wrong, but I wasn't right either. I wish I knew how to fix things." She looked down at THE TAYLORS friendship bracelet they all wore.

Suddenly she had an idea.

There was a knock at her door and her mom popped her head in. "You look great!" she said. "Ready to go trick-or-treating? The girls are meeting you here, right?"

"Change of plans," Teffy said, her heart starting to pound. She had no idea if what she was about to do was going to work, but she had to try. "Mom? Could you take me to pick up the other Taylors? Tay Tay and TS first? There's something we need to do."

Her mom looked at her strangely. "All right. Sure, sweetie."

Teffy swallowed hard. "Just give me ten minutes."

Teffy grabbed her iPad. Her fingers were shaking with excitement and nerves as she sent a text message to her friends.

TEFFYBEN2213@MAIL.NET: Don't leave yet! I'm coming to get you both.

TAYTAY🎉: Why?

TS☻: Everything ok?

TEFFYBEN2213@MAIL.NET: Yes. I'll explain in the car.

Then, in a separate thread, she sent another text. This one was scarier.

TEFFYBEN2213@MAIL.NET: Are you home?

She held her breath and waited. Seconds later, she saw dots pop up.

TAYLOR🕷: Yes. Why?

TEFFYBEN2213@MAIL.NET: Good. Don't go anywhere. We're coming to you.

NINETEEN

Begin Again

Within fifteen minutes, Tay Tay and TS were in the car, and Teffy's mom was driving them over to Taylor's house. Teffy's mom knew about the fight, but Teffy hadn't told her every last detail. She felt too guilty. She knew what her mom would say if she heard how mean Teffy had been.

It was time to change that.

"Can you please tell me what's going on?" Tay Tay whispered. She was sitting in the middle between Teffy and TS. (Teffy had purposefully chosen to sit in the back with her friends so they could talk. She even asked her mom to play the music really loud up front. Her mom didn't ask questions.)

Even in the darkened car, Teffy could see Tay Tay's *Fearless* look was perfect. Teffy loved her silver sparkly flapper dress and TS's "22" look with its black hat, her "22" tee, and biker shorts. They both looked great, but also nervous.

"I texted Taylor," Teffy told them, "and told her we were coming over." She swallowed hard, and her face was warm as she looked back and forth between her two friends. "I know we're mad that she's going to the concert with Hannah, but I also know we're still her friend and it's time we talk about all this."

TS squeezed her hand. Up close, her long red hair smelled like grapes thanks to a curl cream she used. "I'm so glad we're going to Taylor's. I was going to ask you both if we could. It feels weird trick-or-treating without her."

"It feels super weird. And I'm mad but I miss her, and I think it's time we tell her that." Tay Tay played with THE TAYLORS bracelet on her wrist.

"So what do we say?" TS asked worriedly.

"Are we telling her she can't go with Hannah?" Tay Tay wondered. "Or just forgiving her for going with Hannah? Or asking her not to go with Hannah?"

"Maybe we don't bring up the concert at all," Teffy suggested. She'd been thinking about this a lot. "Tay Tay, you said we're all going to screw up sometimes, and we do. But we're still Taylors for life. And I think we need to remind Taylor of that." Even if it was going to kill her to know Taylor was at the Saturday night concert without them.

"Taylors for life. You're right." Tay Tay nodded, the disco ball earrings she'd added to her costume sparkling in the streetlight's glow. "Let's go get our friend back!" The three girls squeezed one another's hands.

When the car stopped in front of Taylor's house, Teffy took a deep breath. Teffy had dropped Taylor off at home before, but never been inside. On the lawn, there were two skateboards and a bike lying on its side next to a soccer net. Five carved pumpkins sat on the porch steps and there was a giant spider tied to the roof of the house and spiderwebs on bushes everywhere for Halloween. Teffy could see the lights on inside Taylor's house. Suddenly she felt nervous.

But she shouldn't have worried. The moment the car had stopped, Taylor stepped onto the porch. Teffy smiled. Taylor was wearing her *Lover* look—a pink boa, a shimmery mermaid-style dress, and booties.

"I'll let you four talk and I'll wait in the car," her mom said.

"Thanks, Mom," Teffy told her as they piled out.

Her heart was in her throat as she approached Taylor on the

walkway. Taylor held her hand up. "Can I say something first?"

Teffy, Tay Tay, and TS nodded.

"I am really sorry about the concert," Taylor said, her voice small. "I want to explain what happened."

"Okay," said Teffy as her heart beat fast. There was so much she wanted to say too, but she didn't want to cut Taylor off.

"Hannah's parents got her and her sister tickets to the concert last year as a birthday gift and said they could each invite one friend," Taylor explained. "Hannah's sister wanted to invite my sister, but my sister wouldn't go unless Hannah invited me, since my sister knew how bad I wanted to go. She didn't know I already made a pact with all of you. So at first I said no." Taylor swallowed hard and stared at her boots. "But then when Hannah and her sister came over last weekend, Hannah told me that she'd talked to her sister and they'd agreed my sister could only have a ticket if I went too. I didn't know what to do." She looked at the others now. "My sister is even a bigger fan than I am and she was begging me. I felt like I had to say yes, but I felt awful about it, and I didn't know how to tell you all the truth."

Teffy felt her stomach churn. Now she felt terrible. "You should have told us."

"I knew Hannah was a mean girl," Tay Tay said, shaking her head.

Teffy could see a lump forming in Taylor's throat.

"I wanted to! I just didn't know how. After our fight, I felt worse." Taylor pushed her dark hair away from her face. "I told my sister what Hannah said to me and said I couldn't go through with it. It felt wrong to go to the concert when none of you could. We made a pact and I ruined it." She took a deep breath. "Then my sister told Hannah's sister what happened, and Hannah's sister told her parents what happened, and then Hannah got in trouble for trying to force me to go with her." She gave a small smile. "Long story short, my sister gets to go, but I'm not going to an Eras concert without you all." She started to cry now. "And I know that doesn't make up for what I did, but I wanted you to know."

TS rushed forward and hugged her. Tay Tay did too.

But Teffy waited. She still wanted to use her voice and this time she wanted to use it to apologize. "Can I say something?" Taylor nodded as she hung on to TS and Tay Tay. "I'm sorry too. I was wrong to make you choose. Whether we made a pact or not, I had no right to kick you out of the friend group." She looked at all their friends. "I was a bad friend too."

"Not as bad as I was," Taylor said, her voice wobbly. "I miss you all so much."

"We miss you too!" TS gushed.

Teffy rushed forward and Taylor pulled her in for a hug. Now all four of them were one big Taylor sandwich, crying and clinging to one another. In the doorway, Teffy spied Taylor's family. When she looked back, her mom was watching too from the car.

"Nothing feels right unless it's the four of us." Teffy sniffed. "I'm sorry I was so mean."

Taylor wiped her eyes. "Actually, I was impressed. I taught you well. Hannah is never going to bother you again." They all laughed. "So, friends again?"

"*Best* friends," Tay Tay assured her.

Taylor grinned through her tears.

"Can we go trick-or-treating now?" Teffy asked.

"Yes!" Taylor said with a laugh. "I want some candy and my mom made us epic trick-or-treat bags. We should use them."

"YES!" said Tay Tay, laughing.

Taylor was suddenly shy. "Can I still come Tay-Gating too, if you didn't find tickets?"

"Yes!" the other three Taylors shouted.

"We did not find tickets," TS told her. "In the last week, tickets got even more expensive."

"What did you decide to do with the money?" Taylor asked. "I'm not asking for any. I just wanted to know."

"It's your money too," Teffy said. "We could split it."

"That feels weird." TS wrinkled her nose, her freckles sparkling in the face glitter she had on. "Maybe we could save it for the next tour and buy tickets then."

"Too far away," said Taylor.

All four girls were quiet for a moment.

"I actually had an idea," TS said. "You know how we said Taylor is always doing things for her fans? And giving money to worthy causes?" They all nodded. "What if we donated the money?"

"A donation inspired by Taylor Swift," Tay Tay said. "I like it."

"I do too," Taylor agreed. "But what should we donate to?"

"What about the Harrison Library?" Teffy suggested. "Mr. Ball said they're trying to save it. They could use all the money they can get."

"Let's do it!" Taylor said emphatically.

"Yes!" Tay Tay and TS agreed.

Taylor looked at the others. "We couldn't have done it without each other." She put her hand out. "One, two, three?"

The other Taylors smiled. They knew exactly what to do.

One by one, they placed their hands on top of one another's as their parents looked on, snapping photos of the four girls, realizing that one fight couldn't end a friendship. Life was about second chances. Taylor sang about them. The Taylors lived them.

"One, two, three . . . Let's go, Taylors!" they all shouted, and threw their hands in the air.

Halloween was officially saved.

TWENTY

Long Live

"The first thing we should do is find a meeting place in case you girls lose each other," said Teffy's mom as they wound their way around the cones and followed the parking attendants to a lot near Victory Field. Since Lucas Oil Stadium's dome wouldn't be open for the show anyway, they were going to a Taylor-themed event happening nearby. Tay Tay's dad got them tickets for the sold-out Baseb-All Too Well: Concert Pre-Party at Victory Field. From what they'd heard on the news, Swifties would be gathering for group sing-alongs, photo booths, bracelet trading, "We Are Never Getting Back Together" nachos, "Fearless" fried chicken, and "Red" velvet cupcakes. Since Tay Tay's dad had also gotten them a parking pass, they were able to Tay-Gate at Lucas Oil with other concertgoers, where there would be merchandise tents, pop-up dance parties, and friendship-bracelet trading happening all over the place. The Taylors planned to make the best of it.

Teffy was bouncing in the front passenger seat. "Let's just park and get out there! I'm so excited."

"Me too! We need to get in line for the merchandise tent," said TS, leaning over the back seat, the two dozen friendship bracelets she was wearing on full display on both arms. (Each girl had a baggie full of additional bracelets to trade too.) "The blue crewneck and the gray quarter-zip sweatshirts keep selling out at shows and they don't sell them on her website."

"I love that blue crewneck," Teffy said wistfully. "It is the one thing I really want to get today."

"Then we will find a way for you to get it," Taylor said with determination. "I want one myself, but if there is only one left, it's yours." The two girls smiled at each other.

"Merch is important, but don't you think we should do another video from the parking lot to Taylor before we get in the line?" Tay Tay asked as she adjusted one of her sparkly disco ball earrings. "So she knows we're here and wearing our Eras outfits and praying by some miracle she sees our video and invites us in to watch the show?"

"Do we really think there's a chance that could still happen?" asked Taylor, who was sandwiched between Tay Tay and TS in the back seat. "I mean, how many tickets do we think Taylor gets for her own shows? Can she just hand out tickets at the last minute if she wants to?"

"I don't know," said Teffy's mom as she pulled into the parking spot and turned off the car. "Girls, I don't want you to get your hopes up, but you can certainly try."

"It can't hurt." Teffy unbuckled her seat belt. "She must have a say in tickets. Doesn't she get to pick who gets the hat? She gave it to Selena Gomez's sister Gracie at one show."

"I know," Tay Tay gushed. "That was so cute. I saw something online that said Taylor's mom walks around and the people who have the best energy and cool costumes get chosen for the hat."

"Well, we definitely have awesome costumes," Taylor said, wrapping her pink boa around her neck.

"Yes we do!" cheered TS, the "22" shining on her tee.

"My mom read some article that said a fan was trading bracelets with Taylor's parents and was later asked to come join them in the VIP area," said Tay Tay as she played with some of the fringe on her flapper dress.

"The VIP area," they all said with a sigh.

Depending on the arena, it appeared to be a raised area on the floor from which celebrities and Taylor's friends and chosen ones got to watch the three-plus-hour show.

But today Teffy had to be happy with the parking lot.

And there was a lot to be happy about.

They were Tay-Gating together. And the listening event at Victory Field sounded cool.

The Taylors were friends again and that was what mattered most.

Everyone piled out of the car while her mom opened the trunk and put out a few chairs they'd used on their last camping trip with the Yoons. Her mom said she was going to hang near the car to read a book and listen to the Taylor music someone was already playing loudly from—was that a radio-station booth?

Teffy hit Tay Tay's arm. "Do you see that spin-y wheel? I think they're giving away stuff! Maybe it's tickets!"

Tay Tay's eyes widened. "Let's go!" She started to dash through the crowd.

"Wait!" Teffy's mom told them. "If I lose you all, I want whoever has a phone to text me once an hour. Agreed?" She looked at Teffy, knowing this phone business was still a sore subject.

"You have your watch now so you can do the same," she added quietly.

"I will," Teffy promised with a smile. Her parents had given her a watch to text on this past week after they'd had a long talk about phones. Teffy had used her voice to explain why she wanted a phone (feeling left out and wanting to keep in touch, not spending hours scrolling mindlessly), and her mom and dad had shared all their fears of having a phone (mainly the mindless scrolling and fears about girls' self-esteem when they spent too much time online). In the end, they all felt like they understood where one another was coming from, and her parents made a deal with her: Every three months, they'd discuss the phone again. Charlie had been given a phone right before seventh grade. Maybe she would be too. Or maybe it would be sooner, but the watch—which allowed texting and calls—was a great compromise. "Wish us luck!"

The girls raced as fast as their legs would take them to the radio-station setup. There was a long line when they arrived, "22" was playing, and fans were singing at the top of their lungs. Teffy had only been to one other concert before, and while it had been fun, fans hadn't really interacted. This wasn't the case at a

Swiftie gathering. People were friendly! They chatted in line for the radio-station booth, traded bracelets, and complimented one another's outfits.

Teffy looked around in wonder at what everyone was wearing. Girls were dressed up in different album-era-inspired outfits, wearing boas, cowboy hats, sparkly dresses, and lots of glitter. There were dads with daughters getting in on the fun with heart-shaped sunglasses, wearing the best T-shirts. (Two Teffy loved: 1. IT'S ME. HI. I'M THE DAD. IT'S ME. 2. DADS ARE SWIFTIES TOO.) Everyone, everywhere, was talking about whether they had tickets or were hoping to score last-minute seats. The stories ranged from people who got into the Ticketmaster queue and paid face value, to others willing to pay several thousand for a seat that night. "Please," she heard one girl crying to her mother. "This person says they can give me a last-minute seat for twelve hundred dollars. Can I take it?" And then them arguing about whether or not the ticket was real. It would all be stressful if Teffy were there alone, but with the Taylors beside her, she was having fun regardless.

Suddenly there was a loud cheer and a siren with flashing lights went off. "Style" played full volume from the speakers.

A girl and a guy started jumping up and down at the front of the line.

"Let's give it up for Kyle and Leyna!" the DJ announced. "They've just won a pair of tickets for tonight's show!"

Everyone clapped and cheered—no bad blood here— applauding two people who, against the odds, had won. Teffy stared at them wistfully. *Maybe we will win too*, she thought.

"Listen," Taylor said to the others. "If I win, two of you are taking the tickets and going to the show." Everyone started to speak over one another. "No buts! We can flip a coin or do Taylor trivia or whatever. But someone is going and it's not me. Not after . . ."

"Hey," said TS softly, and she made heart hands. "That's in the past. We are friends. We are sticking this out together. We all go, or no one goes."

"But if we win tickets, maybe we all will win tickets. Maybe he'll give us five," Teffy said hopefully, knowing it was a dumb idea.

They all gave her a look.

"A girl can dream, can't she?" Teffy started singing "Today Was a Fairytale."

Other people in line joined in.

And then suddenly it was their turns, and one by one, each of the Taylors spun the wheel. Teffy held her breath with each passing spin.

TS went first and won a gift card to a taco shop downtown.

Tay Tay went second and won a radio station T-shirt that said WE HEART TAYLOR SWIFT!

Taylor went third and won a free month of satellite radio for her dad's car.

Teffy's hope was waning. She stepped up as her friends cheered her name. She spun as hard as she could and watched the wheel spin.

The wheel went round and round. Her eyes widened as it started to slow by the tickets symbol.

One tick. Two ticks.

The little flap on the wheel slowed down, teetering between free tickets and an AMC movie theater prize pack. Her heartbeat quickened and a hush grew over her friends as the wheel stopped. Teffy's heart fell.

"An AMC movie theater prize pack! Congratulations!" The DJ handed Teffy a gift card.

Their Eras ticket dreams were officially over.

TWENTY-ONE
Message in a Bottle

"I guess we have to face it—we aren't going to the show," Taylor said dejectedly as they walked away from the merchandise tent three hours later holding everything and anything but the blue crewneck sweatshirt and the gray zip-up that they'd come for.

Teffy looked up at the giant Taylor Swift friendship bracelet hanging on Lucas Oil that New Orleans had shipped here after their own shows and she tried not to be teary.

"No, but we did get the tote bag and the poster," Teffy said optimistically as she texted her mom again to let her know they were off the merchandise line and headed back over to her for the Taylor Swift listening party at Victory Field.

"And matching T-shirts," TS added, trying to be helpful. "And keychains!"

"But no sweatshirts," Tay Tay said, sounding as sad as Teffy. It was the first time all afternoon Tay Tay hadn't been singing at the top of her lungs and goofily dancing around the parking lot. "Guess it wasn't meant to be."

They all stopped in their tracks when they heard a group of girls screaming. "I can't believe we got them! We got last-minute tickets!" one of the girls yelled, and people around them started to applaud.

Taylor tapped one of the girls on the arm. "Hey. Can I ask how much you paid?"

"Two thousand a ticket," said the girl, a glitter star and rainbows on her right cheek. "They're nosebleed, but at least we're inside the stadium. There's almost nothing left this close to showtime."

"Congrats! You're so lucky," Teffy said as another text from her mom came in. She was walking over to check on them. "We're going to the Taylor event at Victory Field."

The girl pulled a bracelet off her arm and handed it to Teffy. "You'll have fun. We did that last night." Her friends called to her. "Bye!"

"Two thousand dollars a ticket," TS said with a sigh, watching the girls run off.

"Okay, no more moping," Tay Tay said, and pulled out her

phone. "We are making Taylor another video from the parking lot." She held up her finger. "No buts. We have to at least try. Everyone, squeeze in. Big energy, people!"

They did as they were told and smiled.

"Hi, Taylor! It's the Taylors!" said Tay Tay. "We are here in the parking lot hoping by some miracle we—"

"Excuse me," a voice interrupted.

The girls turned around.

A cameraman and a reporter were standing behind them. The reporter's microphone said WTTV. That was the station Teffy's parents watched before work in the morning.

"We're doing a report live in a few minutes from the Tay-Gate," he said with a smile, "and I was wondering if I could ask you Swifties some questions on air. Do you think your parents would mind?"

At that moment, Teffy's mom jogged up to them.

"You mean, we get to be on TV?" asked Tay Tay, stepping forward and flipping her hair.

"Yes, and live on the five o'clock news," the reporter said with a laugh. "Is that all right?" He glanced at Teffy's mom for confirmation.

She smiled. "I'm sure your parents wouldn't mind. It's fine by me. What do you say, girls?"

The girls looked at one another and squealed. "Yes!"

"Great! All of you come stand here while I test my mic and this camera light," he said, getting them into position. "And just wait for me to cue you because we're going live in—five, four, three, two . . . Hi, Indianapolis! Glenn Kurt reporting live with four Swifties who are tailgating—or should I say *Tay-Gating*. Quite the different crowd from a Colts game, but fans here couldn't be more excited." He turned to them with the mic, and Teffy's heart started to pound. "Girls, can you tell me your names and where you're from?"

The girls all looked at Tay Tay and TS—the most outgoing of the group.

"We're from Indianapolis and we're all named Taylor after Taylor Swift," TS explained.

Glenn's eyes widened as if he'd hit the jackpot. "Wait. You're all named after Taylor Swift?"

They nodded.

"Our moms and dads are Swifties and named us after her," TS explained. "But none of us met till this year at Harrison Middle School."

Teffy suddenly felt bold. "We were put in the same homeroom so our teacher, Mr. Ball, decided he'd have to call on us using our first names and last name initials. And it was a lot."

Glenn laughed. "So what did you do?"

Taylor stepped forward. "When we wound up at the same lunch table, we started talking about roll call and we decided we would each go by our nicknames instead of 'Taylor.' So it would be easier for people to know who is who. It helps in cheerleading too. We're all cheerleaders for our school team, the Bulldogs."

"Go, Bulldogs!" the Taylors yelled.

A crowd was starting to form around them.

The reporter laughed. "What are your nicknames?"

TS stepped forward. "I'm TS—as in my initials are TS, like Taylor Swift." She looked at Teffy.

"Everyone calls me Teffy. That's what Taylor Swift's brother calls her," Teffy said, and turned to Tay Tay.

"Hi, Indianapolis!" Tay Tay smiled into the camera. "Tay Tay here. My dad gave me the nickname and it stuck even when we moved here this summer from *FLORI-DA!*" She belted the last part out and Glenn laughed.

"And they let me keep being called Taylor," said Taylor. "I'm the youngest of five at my house and always get stuck with hand-me-downs. I didn't want to share my name too." She folded her arms and mock grumbled.

"Love it. So where are you girls sitting for the show?" Glenn asked.

Their faces fell.

"We don't have tickets," TS told him. "We tried everything—radio contests, begging Taylor Swift on social media, fundraising by making friendship bracelets."

Teffy held up her right arm, which was covered in bracelets. "We raised over two thousand dollars making them."

Glenn's eyes popped. "You did?"

"Yep!" Tay Tay said. "We sold them at football games and to busy moms who wanted them for tonight's concert, but in the end . . . we didn't have enough money for everyone to get a ticket. We need five, with us four and a chaperone."

"We made a pact," Taylor told Glenn, and looked at her friends. "We all go or no one goes. We're 'The Taylors.' Friends stick together."

"Wow, that's mature of you girls," Glenn said.

"When we didn't have enough for tickets, we donated the

money," Tay Tay told him. "We wanted to make Taylor Swift proud!" She fist-pumped the air and people who'd gathered round started to cheer.

"Where did you donate it?" Glenn asked, curious.

"The Harrison Library. They had a fire and they're trying to raise money for renovations so it doesn't get torn down," Teffy explained.

"Friends sticking together," Glenn marveled. "What amazing girls you are."

Teffy felt brave. "We've learned from the best—Taylor Alison Swift—who writes the most amazing lyrics and taught us to be good to each other." She looked to her friends.

"And the best part about today is that inside or outside the stadium, we're together," Tay Tay said, and put her arm around Taylor who put her arm around TS who put her arm around Teffy. The girls stood together proudly and beamed.

Glen turned back to the camera. "There you have it, Indianapolis. The power of Taylor Swift, bringing people together."

"And we're out!" said the cameraman as the lights on his camera dimmed.

Glenn shook each girl's hand. "That was great. Thank you!

I hope you girls find a miracle tonight. I think it's amazing you raised all that money and donated it to the Harrison Library."

"Thanks!" TS said.

Glenn asked Teffy's mom for her number in case he decided to do a follow-up piece, and the other girls quickly called their parents to tell them what just happened. They were so energized, Tay Tay led them in a Bulldogs cheer. People who had been watching asked to trade bracelets. By the time the Taylors were done, they were starving and got loaded French fries to share at a food truck. When they finally made their way back to the car and sat in the open trunk, their merchandise purchases tucked away, the excitement of the afternoon died down and reality set in.

"I'm sorry our plan didn't work," Teffy said to the others. "I really thought we'd find a way."

"Me too," said Tay Tay, and squeezed her hand.

"So did I," said TS, who looked teary.

"For a second I thought Glenn had tickets for us, but . . ." Taylor trailed off.

"At least we're together," said Teffy, leaning her head on Tay Tay's shoulder.

"Always." Taylor made a heart with her hands.

Teffy's mom's phone started to ring in her hand and she stared at it, puzzled. "I don't recognize the number."

"Spam," the girls all said in unison.

"Ignore!" said Teffy.

Her mom sent it to voicemail. Then the phone started to ring again.

"It's the same number," her mom said. "Let me just answer it. Hello?"

Teffy watched as her mom listened and a smile broke out on her face. "Yes. Okay. Yes. Four of them. And me. So five!" She laughed giddily.

Teffy's heart started to beat faster. What was happening?

"Is that Glenn?" Taylor asked. "Did he work some magic?"

"Yes, we'll be right there!" Teffy's mom said. "Thank you! They're going to flip." She hung up and looked at the girls in wonder.

"Was that Glenn?" Teffy asked.

"No," her mom said. "That was someone from Taylor Swift's team. They saw you four on the news. They want to give you tickets to watch the concert from the VIP area!"

TWENTY-TWO

The Best Day

The girls started to scream. And hug. Then scream and hug. There were tears. And laughter, and more tears. And they caused such a commotion, people at nearby cars looked at them in wonder. And then there was shouting. Specifically, from Teffy's mom.

"Girls, grab your things! We have to run to the stadium!" Teffy's mom reminded them. "The opening act will be on soon and someone is meeting us to get us inside."

The girls formed a human chain and rushed through the crowded parking lot, screaming and laughing as they ran the whole way to security. Teffy looked up at the massive friendship bracelet hanging on the stadium again and couldn't believe how much had changed in the last few hours. Her mind was buzzing. Had she heard her mom right? Did Taylor Swift's team really reach out? Were they not only going to the concert, but sitting in the VIP area? Was she dreaming?

If so, she didn't want to wake up.

Security had almost no line when they reached the gates. Everyone else was already inside. Teffy could hear the warm-up music playing and the crowd cheering as her mom explained the phone call and someone with a special lanyard appeared at the gate as if by magic. It was a young woman with five lanyards draped over her arm. She placed one over Teffy's mom's head.

"Who is that?" Taylor whispered to the others. "Does she work for Taylor?"

"Girls!" Teffy's mom waved them over. "This is Abby."

"Hi, Abby!" the Taylors said, the nerves in their voices loud and clear.

"Hello to the Taylors!" Abby said. "Loved seeing you on the news. Let me give you your special passes. Do not take these off or give them to anyone else, okay?"

"Are you kidding?" Tay Tay said to Abby and the others. "I'm going to wear this thing till the day I die." They all laughed.

Then Abby handed them each a white wristlet with a light. The ribbon said TAYLOR SWIFT'S ERAS TOUR on it. Teffy felt goose bumps. She knew from watching countless concert videos that the light on the bracelet was synced to the songs and would pulse up in the dark arena when the lights went down.

TS turned to Tay Tay and showed off her wristlet with a squeal.

How is this happening? Teffy wanted to ask, but Abby was already on the move again.

"Follow me, and I'll lead you to your seats," she said.

Abby led the way past the concession stands, past the escalators leading to the higher levels, down the hallway, and into the domed arena. The seats were already full and the arena was loud. Abby walked fast, flashing her pass and saying something to security as they were led onto the floor by the floor seats and then they kept walking. And that's when Teffy heard someone shouting.

"Taylor Perez!"

The girls turned and saw Taylor's sister Maddie waving frantically. She looked even more like Taylor's clone in person, with her long dark hair, deep-set brown eyes, and high cheekbones. "Mom called! I'm so glad you got in!" She was wearing glitter eye makeup and a homemade Swiftie T-shirt and sitting next to someone the girls knew.

Hannah.

Who had brought Greta after all, and was now staring, her mouth open wide as the Taylors walked by her and kept going—all the way to the VIP section. Tay Tay gave the girls a wave. Teffy tried not to smile, but she couldn't help herself. *Yes, Hannah, guess what? We got floor seats too!*

"Here we are," said Abby, stopping at the VIP tent.

It wasn't really a tent so much as it was a tarp covering rows of seats on the floor. There were blockades around it and security to keep anyone from getting inside. But it was prime seating on the floor. Teffy couldn't believe her eyes as security moved a gate and they were ushered to seats in the front row. Strangely, people seemed super excited to see them. "They're the cute girls from the video," she heard someone say as Abby pulled Teffy's mom aside again and whispered something in her ear.

"Girls, I'll be right back," her mom said, beaming so bright she glowed.

The Taylors finally stopped moving and sat down for a second in shock.

"Is this really happening? Someone pinch me," Tay Tay gushed. "No, wait. Don't. I don't want to know for sure."

"It's happening," Taylor said, taking video with her phone of their surroundings. "We are really here! WE ARE SEEING TAYLOR SWIFT!"

The couple next to them laughed and gave a small whoop.

Teffy looked over to see what her mom was doing and saw Abby and her mom talking to security. She wondered what was going on. Were they being booted? Moved? Even if they were told to watch from a concession-stand line, Teffy didn't care. They were inside the arena!

Teffy was getting really emotional. She was just so happy. "I wouldn't want to be here with anyone else."

"Neither would I." Tay Tay sniffed. "I'm so glad we're friends." She opened her arms wide and they group hugged, all sniffling and laughing at the same time.

But then suddenly there was a cheer, and before they knew it, Gracie Abrams was opening for Taylor. The lights were going down and Teffy's mom was coming in beside her and squeezing her arm as they listened to the music, swaying and putting their arms around each other. The seats couldn't be more amazing if they wanted them to. And suddenly everything started moving so fast and after the opening act was off, a massive countdown clock appeared in the center of the stage on the screen, counting down the minutes till Taylor would arrive. Everyone knew exactly what was going to happen. As the clock ticked down and the minutes turned to seconds, the screen turned black, the clock grew bigger and bigger, and people started screaming.

Teffy's heart was in her throat. She felt like she was losing her voice and she'd only started screaming a few minutes earlier. The anticipation was killing her.

Suddenly they heard *her* voice.

And saw the smoke and the massive fans, and the dancers coming down the catwalk.

Teffy's heart started to rev. It didn't matter that she'd seen this on-screen before.

Nothing was like being there live.

Nothing was like hearing people sing along with Taylor, an arena filled with seventy-thousand people all moving as one.

Nothing was like watching it all happen in front of her!

The screaming intensified and then *boom*.

There she was.

Taylor singing "Miss Americana & the Heartbreak Prince."

The Taylors almost lost their minds.

They started to sing too, hearing the songs from a setlist they'd memorized and sang a thousand times before.

With each song and passing era Taylor covered, Teffy was

growing more excited watching her bracelet glow, seeing the show up close, feeling like she was part of something bigger than her. She knew the show was supposed to be three-plus hours long, but it didn't feel like it. Teffy waited for the secret songs. For costume changes. The girls sang to each other, Teffy's mom snapping pictures. Each girl took turns laughing or crying over a favorite tune. It felt like the show had just started when security appeared out of nowhere during "Fearless" and spoke to Teffy's mom.

"This is it!" Teffy's mom motioned to them, filming them as she moved them along. "Girls, come. Quickly now." She didn't seem worried as security moved the barriers again and motioned for the girls.

"Mom, what's wrong?" Teffy panicked.

"Nothing's wrong! Just relax and enjoy the moment." Her mom kept filming.

The Taylors looked at each other wordlessly as security took them up to the edge of the stage. And then in front of the barricades so they were standing against the edge of the catwalk. Teffy's heart started to beat fast, then faster as she looked at the others in wonder, hearing "Fearless" turn to "You Belong with Me" to "Love Story."

She knew what song came next.

She knew why fans got to stand at the edge of this stage.

The other Taylors did too.

"Guys," Tay Tay said, her voice urgent as she started jumping up and down. "GUYS . . ."

"You don't think . . . ?" Teffy whispered.

"No," Taylor said as the security told them to stand at the edge of the stage where there was a step so they could be higher up. "Yes. No. Yes?"

"YES!" TS screamed as "22" started to play and Taylor and her dancers appeared. They were rocking red outfits while Taylor wore the WHO'S TAYLOR SWIFT ANYWAY? EW! tee and the black hat.

The black hat.

Were they getting the hat?

The hat?

No. Yes. No!

Yes?

All four girls started screaming and then quickly their yells turned to singing, and they started doing the hand choreography they knew from watching the Eras Tour movie together so many times.

Taylor and her dancers were singing to *them*.

And the Taylors were singing *back*.

They could see Taylor's smile widen as she approached, her and her dancers moving down the catwalk toward them in one big pack, Taylor skipping toward the front.

Teffy couldn't believe her eyes.

She was coming this way!

Tay Tay was jumping up and down. TS was crying. Teffy wasn't sure if she was going to pass out or leap into Taylor's arms as she approached. The singer whose picture she spoke to, who she admired more than anyone in this world for her lyrics and the way she used her voice, was coming straight toward her. There was so much Teffy wished she had time to say, but she knew the whole thing would only last a moment.

She wanted to enjoy every second of it.

Teffy joined the Taylors in singing as loud as she could, waiting, anticipating when Taylor dropped onto her knees to say hello.

And then it was happening.

Taylor was here! And suddenly she was pulling each girl toward her for a hug.

A hug!

From Taylor Swift!

Teffy wasn't sure if she should laugh or cry, she was so stunned. But she knew what she needed to do. With shaky hands, she slipped her THE TAYLORS friendship bracelet off her wrist and gave it to the singer, *who put it right on her wrist.*

"This is for all of you," their favorite singer in the whole world whispered, pulling the mic away. "Share it, okay?" she said before leaning down and placing her hat atop Teffy's head, then giving the other three Taylors high fives.

And then with a wink and a smile, Taylor stood again and got back to performing the best show Teffy knew she'd ever see in her entire life. Teffy turned to the others in amazement and looked at her mom, who was screaming. TS burst into tears again and Tay Tay started hyperventilating. Taylor was in shock as the security moved them away from the stage again and ushered them back to their seats.

It felt like the entire floor area was looking at them as Teffy held tight to the hat till they were back in the VIP area. For a split second, she wanted to turn and find Hannah in the crowd. She imagined making eye contact with Hannah and smirking, but that wasn't very nice, was it? And it wasn't a Swiftie's style.

Instead, she decided to just focus on her friends and enjoy the moment. Teffy took off the hat and looked inside the rim. She had chills as she spotted Taylor's signature along with the show date and city written inside. She turned the inside of the hat around to show the others. They all screamed some more.

"I can't believe that just happened!" TS said.

"You knew!" Teffy cried to her mom, who hugged her.

"I did! And I refused to ruin the surprise. It was a good one, wasn't it?" her mom said, looking weepy too.

"The best surprise ever!" Teffy looked at the others. "I gave Taylor my THE TAYLORS friendship bracelet," she confessed.

TS gaped as she looked back at the stage. "OMG, Taylor is wearing a bracelet we made her!" The girls screamed again. "We will make you a new one," TS added. "I'm glad you gave Taylor yours."

Teffy removed the hat again—the hat Taylor Swift had just been wearing. "Who's next?"

"Me!" cried Tay Tay, who took a selfie and sent it to her dad. Next it was TS's turn and then Taylor's; each girl posing and taking pictures then taking one photo of them all holding the hat.

Teffy's watch was blowing up with texts from Dad, Charlie. Liam had heard too and said Mrs. Yoon had gotten video of the whole moment on her phone so they could replay it again and again later. Teffy was in total shock. Even more so when Teffy's mom told them Glenn already texted. He wanted to do a follow-up segment on them on the news in the coming week.

But next week was far away.

Right now, they still had the rest of the concert to enjoy.

And they would. Together. Because the Taylors, Teffy knew, were going to be best friends for life.

EVER WONDERED WHAT HAPPENS NEXT?

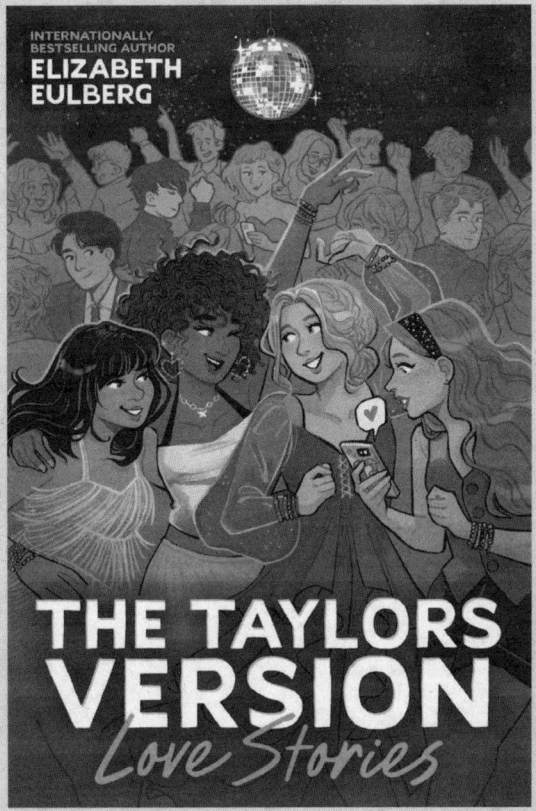

A YOUNG ADULT NOVEL BY ELIZABETH EULBERG

It's four years in the future and Teffy, TS, Tay Tay, and Taylor are starting high school! They plan to crush their freshmen era, but will their friendship change when first loves and school drama enter the mix?

ACKNOWLEDGMENTS

"Are you ready for it?" The answer is a resounding yes! When David Levithan calls you with your dream project, it doesn't matter how many mountains (aka existing deadlines) you have to move to make it happen, you do it. Thank you, David, for trusting me to create a group of middle school characters I would have been besties with. Writing *The Taylors* was pure delight and it's all thanks to you, and editor Maya Marlette. Maya, I am the luckiest author to get to work with an editor who is not only a fellow Swiftie, but one that takes every one of my ideas and makes them better. Someone pinch me! I owe you and David both a zillion friendship bracelets.

Speaking of book besties and fellow Swifties, I couldn't imagine working on this series with anyone other than author Elizabeth Eulberg. Together, we got to create characters that readers will get to watch grow up over the course of our different books. The fact that we've been friends for years only made this collaborative process over Zoom, FaceTime, text messages, and long phone calls even better. Elizabeth, if you're reading this, I'm currently making the heart hands emoji.

Now I'm going to pick up a pair of pom-poms, like the Taylors, to thank Team Scholastic, the biggest cheerleaders of this series. Thank you to Aleah Gorbein, Lizette Serrano, Maisha Johnson, Stephanie Yang, Mary Kate Garmire, Maddy Newquist, Lara Kennedy, Jessica Rozler, Judith Thomas, Brooke Shearouse, and Seale Ballenger for making sure readers everywhere know about these books.

Liz Parkes, I feel like we've been given the greatest gift having you illustrate *The Taylors* covers for both my book and Elizabeth's. They are everything I could have ever hoped for.

Dan Mandel, thank you for always helping me find a way to do all the things I want to do. I feel so lucky to have an agent who always says, "Yes, go for it!" And then helps me make it happen.

Writing a book about Swifties means you talk to a lot of fellow Swifties about your ideas. Thank you to Tiffany Schmidt, Brenda Janowitz, and Joanie Cook for always taking my calls about everything from concert ticket drama to lunchroom drama. And to Elpida Argenziano, Phoebe, and Bella, for opening their home (and their pool!) to me so that I could write this book in "style" under the tightest deadline ever.

To my family—Mike, Tyler, and Dylan—thank you for letting me listen to Taylor music on a constant loop at top volume while I'm writing and for never saying a word when I burn dinner because I was trying to (yet again) do three things at once and manage my deadline.

Finally, to *the* Taylor herself: Thank you for your music, your concerts, and your joyous outlook on life that continues to inspire me and millions of fans.

ABOUT THE AUTHOR

Jen Calonita is the *New York Times* and *USA Today* bestselling author of more than forty books for young readers. Her books have sold more than a million copies and have been translated into fifteen languages. Jen can be found in New York with her husband, two boys, and a feisty chihuahua named Ben Kenobi.

RELIVE *THE TAYLORS* WITH THIS CHAPTER TITLE PLAYLIST OF TAYLOR SWIFT SONGS!

Would've, Could've, Should've

Change

Karma

This is Why We Can't Have Nice Things

Shake It Off

Speak Now

Look What You Made Me Do

Call It What You Want

Everything Has Changed

Breathe

this is me trying

Blank Space

Style

long story short

Don't Blame Me

I Knew You Were Trouble

exile

Bad Blood

Begin Again

Long Live

Message in a Bottle

The Best Day